H

A Stroke of Luck

Kathryn Ellis

James Lorimer & Company, Publishers,
Toronto, 1995

James Lorimer & Company Ltd. acknowledges with thanks the support of the Canada Council, the Ontario Arts Council and the Ontario Publishing Centre in the development of writing and publishing in Canada.

Cover illustration: Daniel Shelton

Canadian Cataloguing in Publication Data

Ellis, Kathryn, 1955–
A stroke of luck

(Sports stories)
ISBN 1-55028-507-6 (bound) ISBN 1-55028-506-8 (pbk.)

I. Title. II. Series: Sports stories (Toronto, Ont.).

PS8559.L558S76   1995   jC813'.54   C95-932674-X
PZ7.E55St 1995

James Lorimer & Company Ltd., Publishers
35 Britain Street
Toronto, Ontario
M5A 1R7

Printed and bound in Canada

Contents

*The author thanks skating coach
Katherine Cruickshank
for her expertise, time, and advice,
as well as the many young skaters
who welcomed me to watch them
practise and compete.*

1

A Strange Day at Millwood Arena

Angie skated to centre ice and struck the pose that started her program. She heard the familiar opening notes of the theme from *The Princess Bride*, and began a graceful spiral, her arms elegantly held out like the wings of a bird, her leg stretched behind her, her back arched in a perfect curve. She was wearing the most gorgeous dress of deep midnight blue velvet, studded with rhinestones that sparkled as she moved through her dazzling spins and footwork. One curling tendril of her strawberry blond hair came loose from her neat braid as she landed jump after electrifying jump. Her final jump, a perfectly executed quadruple axel, brought the crowd to its feet, roaring, as she glided to her final dramatic pose. Pink and red roses rained down on the ice around her. She smiled and waved as she gradually became aware of the smell of bacon.

Angie lay in bed, keeping her eyes closed, willing the dream to continue, but she couldn't help it, she was awake. She continued to lie in bed a few minutes more, savouring the dream, enjoying every last drop of its sweetness. But she didn't really mind having to get up to the smell of bacon, because the smell of bacon meant two things — the taste of bacon was coming next, and it was Saturday, which meant no school, and straight to the rink.

"Angie, breakfast's ready," her mom called.

"Coming!" Angie called back, as she hopped out of bed. She quickly pulled on thick beige tights, a short black skating skirt, and an old T-shirt advertising some long-forgotten movie. She brushed her light brown hair into a ponytail, securing it with a red terrycloth elastic, and wrinkled her freckled nose as she climbed halfway under her dresser looking for her sneakers. Leaving drawers half-open with clothes tumbling out, she was at the breakfast table in less than four minutes, ready to wolf down her mother's wonderful, fluffy, thick pancakes and three slices of bacon. Outside, a few snowflakes drifted across the still-black sky.

"Mom, I need a cheque today," she said through a maple-flavoured mouthful. "We have to put in our entries for Skate Scarborough."

Her mom sighed and tucked a salt-and-pepper strand of her short hair behind her ear. "How much is it for?" she asked.

"Forty dollars." Angie felt bad. She knew it was tough for her mom to pay for all the skating stuff on a cafeteria worker's salary, but she also knew she had a chance at placing in the top ten in her level this year. If only she could do an axel like the one in the dream — not a quadruple, of course, no one could do that, not yet, anyway — just a regular double, but perfectly.

Soon, Angie's mom was dropping her off at the Millwood Arena. It was still dark out, which always gave Angie a slightly sick, shivery feeling, but it was the start of Angie's favourite day of the week. First, there would be several hours of practice time, with about twenty other skaters swirling around her. Then, lunch with her mom and some free time, or a nap. After that, homework (gross!), dinner, some TV or the rest of her homework, and then back to the rink after the Hornets' Saturday night hockey game, when she usually had the whole ice to herself, or almost to herself, from 11:30 until 1:30 to practise her program, work on jumps, or whatever else her coach thought she should be doing. And then tumble, very tired, into bed. It made for a long day, but they had to use the ice when it was available. Still, it wasn't as bad as some hockey teams that practised at three o'clock in the morning.

There was a smell of wet paint as Angie went into the arena, and little wet-paint signs were posted here and there. Through the paint, though, Angie could still smell the ice. It always amazed her that ice actually had a smell — a damp, olden-days smell that always made her feel good. She passed the gallery of photos of skaters from the past, and she made sure to go around, not under, the long ladder leaning against the wall outside the dressing room. Angie wouldn't have called herself superstitious, but why court bad luck if you don't have to?

In the dressing room, Angie carefully laced on her skates, getting the pressure at each point just right, so that she had good support for her ankles, but the flexibility to execute each element properly. Her fingers moved precisely as she looped the laces behind the hooks — it was almost like a ritual. She always zigzagged across the skate, doing up two hooks at the same time for good luck. Some of the other girls were already there, gossiping in the corner, but Angie didn't join in. Several of them, like Paula Stein and Jennifer Chung, went to the same school as Angie, but despite having skating in common, they didn't really hang out together. Angie knew it was partly her fault — they used to ask her to go for a hot chocolate after practice with them, but she'd always declined. She'd always told herself it was because she had to save every penny, but she knew deep down that she felt a little awkward around them, because, well, they were all a lot richer than she was, and they just seemed more sophisticated. They all had Millwood Skating Club sweaters (ninety dollars each), and several practice outfits (at least fifty dollars each), and matching skate bags and garment bags (ninety dollars for the two), and always the most beautiful competition dresses (you don't even want to know).

Jennifer was making a little adjustment to her sock inside her skate, and her glossy black chin-length hair swung forward like a curtain. "I heard there's something up today," she was saying to Paula. "Some kind of announcement."

"I think so," Paula replied, as she twisted her curly dark hair into a bun and wound a scrunchee around it. She examined her face critically in the mirror, for what, Angie couldn't tell. Paula never seemed to have so much as a blackhead on her porcelain skin. Angie would have envied her — she was rich, she was pretty, and her parents were not only her coaches, they were Bob Stein and Céline Leger, two-time Canadian Pairs champions — but it wasn't worth wasting the energy on, as far as Angie was concerned. "I couldn't get out of my parents what it is, but I'm pretty sure something's up," Paula concluded. "I mean, besides Jason."

Curious about the announcement and wondering who Jason might be, Angie hurried out to the ice and removed her skateguards, setting them on top of the boards. She began warming up by stroking — taking long, gliding steps around the ice, going faster and faster, until she was nearly out of breath. She waved to her coach, Ginny, who was standing in the penalty box bundled up to the chin, and she passed, or was passed by, the other skaters on the ice. After a few minutes of limbering up, she skated backward for a while, then tried a spiral or two. Just as she was about to begin practising a spin, the P.A. system clicked on.

"Hi gang, it's Dave here," came the voice of the club president. "Can I get you all to come over to this side of the rink? I've got a couple of things to tell you." So there *was* a surprise announcement.

Angie finished her spin — it was a little off centre — and joined the other skaters gliding over to the side of the rink. As they waited for Dave to come down the stairs, Angie noticed an unfamiliar face among the skaters. It was a boy, a kind of shy-but-friendly-looking boy, with carrot-coloured hair and freckles.

"Two things," Dave began when he reached the ice. "I'd like you all to meet Jason McNeil. He's just moved here from Orangeville, and I hope you'll make him feel welcome."

Everyone looked at the new boy, whose face flamed beet red, an unfortunate combination with his carrot-red hair. Angie felt for him, and tried to smile encouragingly, but he didn't notice. Behind her, she heard Jennifer whisper, "Orangeville — I wonder if they named it after his hair," and Paula's snicker. Angie couldn't keep her smile from turning to a slight smirk. It *was* funny, even if it was kind of mean.

Dave was continuing. "Big news, however, on the subject of Skate Scarborough. You're all too young to remember the skating of Elizabeth Simon, but I'm sure you know who she was. Well, long before winning the World Championship for Canada, she won Skate Scarborough. When she died last year, she was a very rich lady, and in her will, she left a scholarship fund. Each year, the gold medalist in each of the ladies' categories will win a year's free coaching."

A murmur of amazement ran through the skaters. No one had ever heard of anything like this before. The coaches were all smiling indulgently. Obviously they'd already been told.

"The silver and bronze medalists will also win partial scholarships," Dave continued. "Now several of you stand a chance of receiving these scholarships, so I hope you'll all skate your best. For those of you just entering the competition for the first time, don't worry. It's set up so that they can be given every year. You'll want to work hard too, so that you have a chance at the scholarships in future. Now go on, and skate hard!"

Angie couldn't believe her ears. A year's free coaching! That was, like, thousands of dollars! "Ginny," she said excitedly to her coach as they met by the boards, "do you think there's a chance *I* could win that?"

"Angie, I think you should aim for top ten, like we talked about. It's only your second year at this level of competition. I don't want to see you thinking of winning at all costs. I want to see you thinking of skating your best, and then pushing that best to better than best. Okay?" was Ginny's reply. Ginny was always so calm and sensible. Too calm and sensible.

Angie nodded, but in her heart, she made a promise to herself to finish in the medals.

Ironically, practice was horrible. Angie couldn't seem to concentrate and kept wobbling on edges, putting her foot down — simple, baby stuff she should be over by now. She practised some spins, a complicated bit of footwork, and then it was time to try some jumps. The dreaded double axel. It didn't matter to Angie that everyone had trouble with it. It only mattered that *she* had trouble with it. Part of what made it so hard was the forward takeoff. Like most skaters, she always found it easier to jump when she was travelling backward — something to do with the centre of balance, Ginny said. Then, even though it was *called* a double, it was really two and a half turns — more rotation than a normal double — so you landed going backward. *And* you landed on the opposite foot you took off from, just to make things complicated.

Whichever one of these things Angie was having trouble with today, she couldn't seem to land even one double axel properly. Most times she fell, which wasn't so much painful as it was frustrating, although she was starting to feel a bit beaten up. She might as well have walked under that stupid ladder.

"Try it again," called Ginny. "Pull your arms in tighter."

Angie didn't want to try it again, she was getting tired of falling, but she knew that without practice, practice, and more practice, she'd never get it right. She skated backward, building up speed, then step and jump, and turn, and — "Ow!" she barked, as a sharp pain hit her foot, and she tumbled in a heap on the ice.

Ginny came skating over quickly. "What is it?" she asked, as Angie held her foot.

"I got my feet tangled," Angie explained. She was afraid to look and just went on holding her foot. "I stabbed myself with my blade, I think."

"Let's see," said Ginny. A couple of other skaters had stopped practising and came to see what was happening, but most went on with their routines.

Reluctantly, Angie took her hand off her skate. There was no blood.

"Let's see," Ginny said again. "You've cut your skate a little, but it'll be okay," she commented, undoing Angie's laces. "There's no blood," she said, examining Angie's foot. "You'll probably have a bruise for a little while. You'll live."

Angie smiled ruefully.

"Never mind," said Ginny. "You're just having an off day. Time's almost up, so why don't we call it quits for now?"

Normally, Angie would beg for just one more minute on the ice. One day, her mother always said, she'd be sucked up by the Zamboni. But today she felt jangled and relieved to escape, and she went straight for the dressing room, near tears — of frustration more than pain.

Alone in the dressing room, she took off her skates. She examined her bruised foot again. It really was fine, just a little tender. After carefully wiping the blades dry, she began to put away her skates. Suddenly, from the corridor, came a scraping noise, a sharp squeal, and then an enormous crash.

2

The New Kid from Orangeville

Skates in hand, Angie ran to the corridor. From the door of the dressing room, she saw the long ladder she hadn't walked under, now lying on the floor. Paula, looking terrified, was sitting on the floor beside it, and the rest of the skaters and a couple of coaches were standing around, amazed. Paula's dad was crouched down, asking if she was all right, and Dave was approaching at a run, inquiring what had happened.

"I'm okay," said Paula shakily. "I … I'm not sure what happened. The ladder just fell over. I jumped out of the way, and lost my balance."

"Did anyone else see it?" someone asked. A few people shook their heads; no one answered.

"Did *you* see anything, Paula?" asked Paula's dad.

"Well … " Paula thought a moment. "I thought I did see someone — just out of the corner of my eye."

"Who else was out in the hall?" Dave asked, looking around the group.

No one owned up.

"Was anyone off the ice?"

"I was," said Angie. "But I was inside the dressing room, so I didn't see anything. Sorry."

"Well, we'll have to give that ladder a careful check," said Dave, pulling the ladder over to the wall and laying it flat. "You sure you're okay?"

Paula nodded. "It didn't hit me or anything."

But it could have, everyone was thinking. Angie thought about how it could just as easily have fallen on her, she was the last one through the corridor before Paula. She looked up to see Jennifer giving her a funny look.

"Been a bit of a bad luck day," commented Dave, "between Angie and Paula. Someone must have walked under this thing."

A few people smiled. Paula was one of them, but her smile was guilty. "Actually, I did, earlier," she admitted. "I was trying to prove I wasn't superstitious. I think maybe I am now."

Everyone laughed, a little nervously, and the crowd began to disperse.

***

That night, Angie yawned as she laced up her skates. The hockey game was over — the Hornets had won — and the spectators were gone. The players were leaving in noisy clumps and the Zamboni was chugging around the ice surface. Those hockey guys sure knew how to chew up the ice. The smell of french fries and vinegar had pretty much wiped out the wet-paint smell of earlier in the day.

When she went out onto the ice, Angie found that this was not one of the nights she'd have the whole rink to herself. Both Paula and the new boy, Jason, were warming up, stroking around the arena. Paula's parents were standing by the edge of the ice, and they waved to Angie as she glided across the white surface. As Angie finished her warmup, she thought about how great it would be to have Paula's parents. Although Bob and Céline had never won a World Title or an Olympic medal, they were still well remembered for their incredible grace and unity as skaters. A large photograph of them hung in the lobby of the arena. Not that Angie would trade them for her own mom, of course. But they were way more expensive than Ginny, and Paula just got them for free.

Angie skated over to the booth to put on her *Princess Bride* music. Jason skated past her, very fast, and said, "Hi Angie, how's your foot?" He seemed to be quite a good skater, Angie noticed, very surefooted. But then, he was at least two years older than Angie. Fifteen, or maybe even sixteen.

"A little sore," she called after him. "Better, though."

"Good!" he yelled back, now at the end of the ice.

Her music began to play, and she started her opening spiral. Her foot was still sore, but not enough to keep her from skating. But then, her feet would have to be gone altogether for that! Even though she was tired, she was determined to put in a good workout to make up for her lousy morning. Then out of the corner of her eye, she noticed something that startled her. Jason had lifted Paula high over his head. "Good, good," Bob was encouraging them. So that was why Jason had come all the way from Orangeville. He was going to be a pairs partner for Paula, and he was getting coached by the very best. Well, well.

Angie knew she should be concentrating on skating, not on what the others were doing. She raised her back foot a little higher, straining for that perfect, bird-like arc in her spiral. In the footwork section, she remembered to keep her chin up — it was so tempting to look down at her feet! — and her hand in a perfect, balletic curve. And as she spun, she tried to hold onto that imaginary wire that ran from the top of her head through her middle, boring a hole in the ice. Ginny had said not to practise any jumps until her foot was back to normal, but she couldn't resist trying the axel just once. Landing on her sore foot, she went sprawling across the ice, but she scrambled up as quickly, vowing to listen to her coach in future. Back to the spins. Practice, practice, and more practice. It was hard work, but Angie couldn't imagine anything she'd like to do more. In what seemed like mere minutes, the two hours were up.

When the buzzer sounded, Angie grabbed her sweatshirt and skateguards from where she'd left them and headed for the dressing room. She unlaced her skates, two hooks at a time, as Paula and her mother came in.

"Well *that's* going to take some work," Céline was saying, a little crossly. "Just because he's lifting you up doesn't mean you're a sack of potatoes. You have to work too."

"I know, Mom," sighed Paula.

Angie left the dressing room. In the corridor, she noticed her mom was busy talking to Dave, so she sat down on a bench to wait. A moment later, Jason came out of the men's dressing room and glanced around.

"I guess my mom's not here yet," he said.

Angie smiled, and made room for him on the bench.

"So you're from Orangeville?" she asked him, as he sat down beside her. What a stupid thing to say! She could have kicked herself. What was he going to do, say no?

"That's right," Jason replied.

"Um, how do you like Toronto so far?" Angie asked, looking for a better conversation starter.

"Not much, to tell you the truth," he said. "At home, there's fields, and it's not far to go out to the woods. Here, it's nothing but concrete. No wonder everyone seems crazy. There's no outdoors."

Angie looked at Jason with some surprise. She'd lived in Toronto all her life and loved it. Besides, there was lots of outdoors, parks and ravines and everything. And wasn't it kind of rude for a newcomer to criticize?

"So you're partnering with Paula, eh?" she asked, mostly to change the subject.

"Maybe. Probably. I came to get coached by Bob and Céline." Jason indicated the life-size picture of the duo on the opposite wall. "Paula and I are trying it out. I think it will work out, though."

Thinking of Céline's remark about potatoes, Angie wasn't sure what to say next. Finally, she said, "Good."

A few moments later, Jason spoke. "Hey, I'm sorry if I seemed rude, before. I guess I'm just kind of homesick."

"Did you have a lot of friends in Orangeville?"

"Yeah, but mostly I miss my little brother."

"Didn't he come here with you?"

"No, he's in Orangeville. My dad works there so he had to stay. It seemed better for my brother not to change schools. My mom and I came here for the skating. It seems strange, being only half a family."

"I'm only half a family. Just me and my mom," said Angie brightly.

"Where does your dad live?" Jason asked.

"I don't know. He left when I was really little. I don't remember him." Angie was surprised at herself for saying so much to someone who was practically a stranger. "My mom says he lives in a trailer park in Florida, but I think she just says that to make me feel better." There was a brittle tone to her voice that she hoped Jason hadn't noticed.

"Geeze," replied Jason. "Sorry, I shouldn't have asked."

"No, it's okay. I don't mind at all," said Angie, trying to put the smile back into her voice that she must have lost somewhere back there.

Before she could think of a better conversation — she really was very bad at this — Jason's mom arrived, and the two said goodbye.

***

When she arrived at the rink after school on Monday, Angie watched the end of the hockey practice with the others. Jennifer and Paula were giggling together in the penalty box, and Angie noticed they were eating french fries, generally forbidden by Paula's parents. An open packet of salt drifted to the floor, spilling its contents onto the concrete. Angie wondered why the girls didn't toss a pinch over their left shoulders, to counter the bad luck. When Jason arrived he waved to them. Soon the buzzer sounded, and Angie went into the dressing room to lace up her skates while the Zamboni smoothed the ice. Paula came in a moment or two later.

"Where's Jennifer?" asked Angie, idly.

"Oh, she's got her skates on already," said Paula, reaching into her bag for her own. "Hey!" she suddenly called out.

Angie and the others in the dressing room looked up.

"My laces are missing!" Paula held up the skates, and sure enough, both laces were gone.

"Did you leave your bag somewhere?" asked one of the little girls.

"I set it down in the hall when I was buying — I mean Jennifer was buying french fries in the canteen," said Paula, "but I was only in there for a minute. There *were* some hockey players — at least I *think* they were hockey players — around, though," she added, thoughtfully.

"Don't you have a spare pair?" Angie was anxious to get out onto the ice.

Paula dug around in her bag. "No," she said. "I thought I did."

"Remember, you broke one, a couple of weeks ago," said Tiiu, one of Paula's crowd.

"You're right, I forgot. Those *were* my spares. *Now* what am I going to do? I can't skate if I can't keep my skates on!" Paula's voice was getting more and more frantic.

After a moment, Tiiu piped up. "Well, here, have my spares. You can pay me back."

"It was the salt," said Angie.

"What?" asked Paula.

"The salt you spilled," said Angie. "From your french fries. You didn't toss a pinch over your left shoulder."

"You mean, Jennifer's french fries. I didn't spill any salt," said Paula, pointedly.

"What's wrong?" came Céline's lightly accented voice from the doorway.

"My laces are missing. Tiiu's lending me her spares," Paula explained.

"Well, hurry up, you're wasting ice time," said her mother in an exasperated tone of voice.

Angie didn't wait to hear any more. She didn't want to lose one second of skating if she could help it. She got to the ice just as the Zamboni was chugging off.

Angie had nearly warmed up by the time Paula finally made it to the ice.

Practice went well. Even the double axel was coming along.

"Good girl!" shouted Ginny from the sidelines, as Angie tossed off a beautiful one — smooth takeoff, a tight, high spin in the air, and she absolutely nailed the landing. She was feeling pretty good by the time the session was over.

"Keep skating like that," said Ginny, "and you'll make the top ten *easily*."

"Really?" asked Angie, trying to push back the exciting thought that crept again to the forefront of her mind. "Do you think I might win a medal?"

"Well, now, don't get ahead of yourself," cautioned Ginny. "You've still got a lot of work to do." That was Ginny, calm and sensible as usual.

"I will," Angie assured her. I will. I will. I will work so hard nobody will believe it. I will do nothing but work hard from now until the competition. There will be nothing in my head but skating, Angie vowed to herself as she slipped on her skateguards and headed for the dressing room.

As soon as she walked in, conversation abruptly stopped. She glanced at the group of girls around Paula, who all suddenly began talking about different things.

So, they were talking about me, thought Angie, and she wondered what they were saying.

Paula, Jennifer, and Tiiu breezed past as Angie was still getting her skates off.

"Bad things come in threes," said Tiiu, primly. Angie thought she always seemed a bit prim, with her white-blond hair pulled severely into a bun, and her buttoned-up-to-the-neck pink cardigan.

"Then they're done," said Paula. "Angie's foot, the ladder, and the laces."

"*If* you count Angie's foot," said Jennifer, as the three of them wandered out the door.

Now what on earth could she have meant by that, wondered Angie, as she undid her laces together, two hooks at a time, the way she always did, for good luck.

3

Skating Dresses

Angie's feet crunched on the snow beneath her boots as she walked home in the fading light. It was almost her favourite time of day, the sun a huge orange ball on the horizon, the streets quiet as most people were home having dinner, the houses with their lights on. Some still had their curtains open, and you could see inside. It gave her a funny feeling, halfway between independent and lonely. At home, her mom was probably stirring up some hamburger helper or something.

She hadn't thought too much about Paula's laces disappearing until now. It really was peculiar. She knew Paula couldn't have taken them out herself and forgotten about it. It took time to unlace a pair of skates, you'd notice you were doing it. But who else would have taken them out? And why? Was there a thief in the skating club? That was a nasty thought. Paula had mentioned seeing hockey players near her bag, and they would use skate laces. Or was someone trying to play a joke on Paula? If so, it wasn't very funny. And what did Jennifer mean when she said, "if you count Angie's foot"? Maybe she just meant that Angie's foot didn't happen to Paula. But the way she put the emphasis on *if* sounded like she meant something more. Did she think *Angie* had played a joke on Paula? But why would she? Oh, it was all too complicated, she sighed, as she climbed the iron stairs to her and her mom's cozy (Mom's word), squinchy (Angie's word) apartment.

"Angie," called her mom from the kitchen in an excited voice, "look on the table. You've got mail."

Angie pulled off her boots and hung her coat on a hook on the wall. When she came into the kitchen and saw the lavender envelope in the middle of the table, she grinned. A lavender envelope could only mean one thing — a letter from her grandparents. And a letter from her grandparents addressed to Angie meant Gran had been having good luck at Bingo again. She picked up the envelope and tore it open.

"'Dearest Angie,'" she read aloud to her mother. "'Pop and I are coming in for your big competition, and we wanted to make sure you'd look respectable for us. Somebody up there must like you, because I've been having such a streak of luck at the Bingo. So I've sent you some money for a nice skating dress.' Oh, Mom, it's two hundred dollars! Can I really spend it on a dress?"

"That's what Gran sent it for, so I guess you can," replied Angie's mother, smiling.

"You know what I want?" Angie babbled on excitedly, remembering the dress from her dream. "I want dark blue velvet, with a double skirt, white underneath, and rhinestones, for sparkle!"

"Well, I don't know if two hundred will cover that, but we can see."

"And shimmery tights."

"That, I think we can do," laughed her mom.

***

That night, Angie tossed and turned in her bed, unable to sleep. Usually, she put herself to sleep by visualizing herself skating through her program. It was soothing, and Ginny believed that it helped in performance. So did Angie, but tonight she was overexcited about the new dress she was going to buy. She imagined the soft texture of the velvet, and how luxurious it would feel. She pictured herself skating, and as she spun, the white underskirt flashing out from under the dark blue. But most of all, she pictured the rhinestones, glittering like winter stars — not tons of them, not gaudy, but classic, shooting light into every corner of the arena. But as the night got later, and there were hardly any human sounds in the world, her thoughts wandered back to the two strange things that had happened to Paula. The ladder must have been an accident, although it was odd that it had fallen just as Paula walked by. And the missing laces were the work of either a thief or a prankster. Laces don't just walk off. There was probably no connection. It was odd, though, how Angie had bruised her own foot just minutes before the ladder had fallen, when nothing like that had ever happened before. That was that strange day when they had announced the scholarships and — Jason. It was Jason's first day at the arena. But Jason hadn't caused Angie to hurt herself. Still, if he was the culprit, it might have given him the idea to sabotage Paula by knocking over the ladder and hiding her laces.

But why on earth would Jason want to sabotage Paula? Surely he wanted to have her as a partner and get coaching from former champions too. And surely Paula would have recognized *him*, if that was who she had seen out of the corner of her eye. It made no sense. On the other hand, Jason had mentioned that he was homesick. Why did Paula leave the ice early? And where was Jason then? No, no, it couldn't be anything like that, surely it was just a coincidence … And that was where Angie's mind left the mystery as she finally tumbled off into sleep.

Angie woke up exhausted but managed to drag herself out of bed. As she walked to school, she thought again about Jason. He seemed like such a nice guy; the idea that he might harm Paula just seemed to go against the grain in so many ways. Still, she didn't really know him. At last, Angie decided to have a conversation with him and see whether she could find out anything.

School dragged by that day at a horribly slow pace, but finally, the three o'clock bell rang. Angie had spent most of the day paying no attention to any of her classes, thinking about how she would manage to tackle Jason, but as luck would have it, she practically bumped into him outside the school, where he was unlocking his bike.

"Hi there. How's it going?" Angie asked.

"Oh, hi, Angie. What's new?"

"Not much. Going to the arena?"

"Yeah," said Jason. "I'll walk with you."

"You actually ride a bike in winter?"

"I ride a bike anywhere, anytime, except in a blizzard," Jason replied. "It's a great workout, and I hate waiting for buses."

"I guess," said Angie, doubtfully. "Weird about Paula's skate laces yesterday, wasn't it?"

"I know," agreed Jason, emphatically. "I wonder who would play a trick like that?"

"You think it was a trick?" asked Angie. How, exactly, did he know?

"What else could it have been? She lost more than five minutes of ice time. Somebody have it in for her?"

Well, that didn't sound like the response of a guilty person. Still, he might be a good liar.

"Not that I know of," replied Angie, carefully.

"Well, who knows?" said Jason, quite casually. "I'm really enjoying this pairs thing. I've never really skated pairs before. You have to build up so much — I don't know — trust between each other. It's a delicate thing to do. But it's interesting." He grinned at Angie.

Well, that *certainly* didn't sound like the confessions of a lace-snatcher. Still, Angie couldn't be sure.

It wasn't long before they arrived at the rink, and Jason stopped to lock his bike while Angie went in.

The first thing she noticed was that something was definitely wrong. Once more, Paula was at the centre of the commotion, with the other girls squealing in outrage around her. They turned and looked at Angie as she came in.

"What's going on?" she asked.

"*Somebody* played another trick on Paula," said Tiiu, with a nasty edge in her voice.

"What happened?"

Paula held up her skating dress, one that Angie had always admired, a simple white spandex outfit with a double skirt and black trim around the cuffs and neckline. But now, the top of the front and most of one sleeve were stained a bright purple.

"Somebody dumped grape juice in my bag," said Paula. "That stuff doesn't come out."

"*Somebody* has a sick sense of humour," said Tiiu.

"Well, don't look at me, I just got here," replied Angie, irritated.

"Now what am I going to do?" moaned Paula. "I have to wear something to skate in."

"You'll just have to wear it," answered Tiiu. "Dry it under the hand dryer."

"It's *ruined*!" cried Paula. "Ruined. My mom will kill me." The two girls went into the washroom, which was just off the dressing room, to take care of the damp, stained dress.

Angie quickly got changed and laced up, two hooks at a time. This was getting to be more than coincidence. Somebody really did have it in for Paula. Taking the laces wasn't very nice, but the grape juice was just plain mean. As she went out the door of the dressing room, she almost collided with Jason.

"Oh, Ange, can you tell Paula I'll be out in a sec?"

"She's late, anyway. Someone spilled grape juice on her dress. She's drying it off."

"You're kidding!" replied Jason. "What's going on around here?"

Angie just shrugged, and Jason went into the men's dressing room to get changed. But as Angie began warming up, she kept pondering what had happened. Obviously Jason was in the clear, since he'd just arrived with her. And the grape juice was probably done in the dressing room, so it was unlikely to be a boy. Well, three bad things had happened to Paula now, so Angie decided to put it all out of her mind and concentrate on skating.

And skate she did. Her centre was dead on, and she spun like the blade on a food processor. She nailed every jump, even the double axels. Over and over, she jumped. Step, push off, arms tight, spin, spin, and firm landing on her other foot, arms out, free leg high, ready for her next element. Her footwork was crisp, and her edges sharp and smooth. Oh, if only she could skate like this at Skate Scarborough!

"Excellent, today. Terrific," exclaimed Ginny at the end of practice. The buzzer sounded to warn the skaters to clear the ice for the Zamboni, but Angie lingered, trying a few simple waltz jumps and a long, graceful spiral as she glided off the ice before the oncoming Zamboni. Finally, the last one on the ice, she grabbed her guards and sweatshirt and went back to the dressing room. The other girls were already in their street shoes, and Paula had changed into her clothes. Most of the girls just stayed in their skating dresses, changing once they were home, but Paula clearly didn't want the purple-stained dress any more. None of them spoke to Angie as they left.

The white dress was left behind, dangling from a hook in the empty dressing room like a flag without a breeze, like an accusation.

4

Alarm Bells on Finland Street

Life was not nearly so dramatic for the next few days. Nothing new happened to Paula, or Angie, or anyone else. The white dress still hung limply in the women's dressing room, clearly abandoned by Paula. Angie often had lunch with Jason at school, went to the rink, and did her homework. She was skating well, though she was still inconsistent with the axel.

About a week after the grape-juice incident, Angie came out of the arena to find Jason leaning on his bike, waiting for her.

"There you are," he said to her. "Which way are you headed?"

"I'm just on my way home," she said. "I live on Millwood, just a few blocks along."

Jason walked his bike alongside her. "The thing is, I'm not sure how to tell you this, or even whether I should," he began, rubbing his hand on the back of his neck.

"What?" asked Angie, a little alarmed.

"Well, I heard this rumour today, and I thought you should know. I mean, I think you should know. I don't know."

"What?" asked Angie again, more than a little curious.

"Well, I think some people think you're the one playing the practical jokes on Paula."

"What?!" cried Angie, for a third time. "How could they think that? Who thinks that?" This was terrible!

"Hey, *I* don't think it, at least, you didn't, did you?"

"How can you even ask me that?"

"Sorry, sorry. I know you're not the type."

"Darn right I'm not," said Angie, firmly. "But why do they think I am?"

"Well, I guess, because you're trying to upset her."

"Upset her?"

"Well, they say that if she does badly you have a chance of winning a medal at Skate Scarborough. They say that Jennifer will probably get gold, like she did last year, and that girl, April, from Thornhill, and Paula and you are probably the biggest contenders — plus a girl from Ottawa, Keniesha or something."

In spite of the unpleasantness of the accusation, Angie was a little bit thrilled that the others considered her a possible medalist, and that Paula saw her as a threat. But she was also furious. "I stand a chance at a medal, even *with* Paula in the competition," she snapped. "I don't need to resort to mean tricks to beat Paula. Anyway, why wouldn't I go for Jennifer, then?"

"Tricks wouldn't work on Jennifer."

"No, I suppose not," mused Angie. She thought about Jennifer's single-minded determination. "Nothing would get to her. But you're right. If someone did want to upset Paula, this would be a way to do it. I've never thought she has the concentration that Jennifer does."

"I know what you mean," Jason agreed, looking a little concerned.

"The pairs thing isn't going well?"

"I wouldn't say that. But I'm glad you said that, about Paula being upset, because something's off with her, and that's probably it."

"Off?" prompted Angie.

"Don't forget, I didn't know her before the pranks started, so I don't know what she's usually like," Jason continued. "Sometimes, it seems almost like she doesn't want to be there. I thought maybe she didn't like *me*. But you're right — it's the pranks, it must be. I sure hope whoever it is stops." Jason looked at Angie.

Was he trying to tell her something? Did he really suspect her, too? "I didn't do it," she told him. "You believe me, don't you?"

"Of course I do," said Jason quickly. Angie was pretty sure he was telling the truth. The two were standing at the bottom of the iron back stairs to Angie's apartment.

"Well, thanks for telling me, anyway. I'm with you. I hope whoever's doing it has finished."

"Don't you want to find out who it really is?" asked Jason.

"Quite honestly, I couldn't care less," she replied.

"But don't you want to clear your name? I mean, you don't want it spreading all through skating that you've got a mean streak, do you?"

Angie sighed. "I suppose you're right," she agreed, but it made her feel tired. She was supposed to be concentrating on skating, not playing Nancy Drew.

"I'll help you, if you like."

"Just my luck," Angie replied. "As if I don't have enough to do with everything else, I have to be a detective now, too."

"I'll help, really," said Jason.

Angie looked up at him, squinting one eye against the setting sun. She had never really noticed before how interestingly attractive orange hair could be. It was probably a trick of the light. "Thanks," she said, her mouth curving into a smile. "Um, I've got to get in," she went on, suddenly shy. "Meet me at lunch tomorrow. We can make a plan."

"Okay," said Jason. "See you then." He swung a leg over his bike and pedalled off across the snowy sidewalk, bumping down onto the road from the curb.

Angie's feet made the iron staircase ring as she climbed the stairs, contemplating the tossed salad of emotions she was feeling. Mad. Sad. Glad. She went in the back door, and as she was pulling off her boots, she noticed the familiar yellow label of an empty can of pea soup in the blue recycling box. Not a good sign.

Sure enough, when she came into the kitchen, she could smell the pot of soup steaming on the stove, and there was her mom at the kitchen table, surrounded by paper, hurriedly shoving a kleenex into the pocket of her sweater. She always made pea soup when they were feeling especially poor, because it was cheap.

"Hi, honeybun," said Angie's mom, looking up and smiling brightly. Her eyes were watery and red, and her short grey-brown hair looked like she'd been running her fingers through it until it stood on end.

"Oh, Mom," Angie replied, dropping into the other chair at the table. "It'll be all right. You always figure something out."

But her mom shook her head. "I don't know, honeybun, I don't know how we'll do it this time. I just can't see …" She broke off, shaking her head again. "Well," she said, with a brittle cheerfulness, "let's have some soup, all right?"

"I'll get it." Angie jumped up, anxious to be busy. She always felt so guilty when money trouble came up, because she knew that if only they didn't have all her skating expenses they would be, well, maybe not rich, but at least getting by. While her mom tidied away the bills and papers, Angie carefully ladled the soup into the bowls that were waiting on the

counter and carried them, one by one, to the table. She put out
a plate of soda crackers, and got the jar of Dijon mustard out
of the fridge. It was her mother's little indulgence, Dijon
mustard, she loved it on all kinds of things — chicken, sau-
sages, stirred into pea soup. It was more expensive than the
regular kind, but her mom always justified it by saying, "I
only use a little bit at a time. It's just such a nice treat." Angie
couldn't fathom it, she hated the stuff.

Angie's mom picked up the jar of mustard and looked at
it, then covered her mouth with her fingers and was very still
for a moment.

Angie could tell her mom was on the verge of tears, and
Angie felt kind of like crying, too. "Don't be ridiculous," she
said fiercely, to keep the tears from bursting out. "Eat the
whole stupid jar. You could have fifty jars of it for the cost of
a pair of my skates."

Her mom swallowed, and tried to smile. She took Angie's
hand. "You're my angel, you are. So," she went on brightly,
"how was skating today?"

After all this, Angie couldn't tell her about the rumours
Jason had warned her about. She just said, "Fine. I think my
axel is getting a little better. More consistent." The crisis had
passed, and conversation was normal as they finished up the
soup — which Angie would probably have liked if it weren't
always associated with bad times — and cleared up the
dishes. Finally, Angie put the unopened jar of mustard back in
the fridge and went to her room to do her homework.

But sitting at her desk, she couldn't concentrate on anything. She looked around at the piles of clothes and other
stuff, and the posters of her idols on the walls. Kurt Brown-
ing. Elvis Stojko. Josée Chouinard. Elizabeth Manley. She
even had an autographed picture of Vern Taylor, who wasn't
that famous anymore, but he was the first skater to land a
triple axel in competition, back in the seventies. He some-

times coached at Millwood. Of course, now lots of people could do a triple axel. It was all pretty daunting when she thought about the work she had to do just to master the double.

And then there was that rumour. She really was upset about the others thinking she could have played mean tricks on Paula. She didn't especially like Paula, but she wouldn't do something like that to anyone. And her mom was way more worried about money than Angie ever remembered seeing her. The thoughts chased each other around in her head like a trio of squirrels, leaping and darting, and making each other run. And then they collided, sickeningly. She could deal with all three problems with just one action. She could quit skating. She wouldn't need to master the axel. It wouldn't matter then what the others said about her. Plus if anything else happened, they'd know it couldn't be her, and she'd be off the hook. And what it would do for their finances! The coaching alone was the killer, and she knew that Ginny didn't even charge for all the time she spent with her. And then there was ice time, and skates, and costumes.

But to give up skating! It was almost more than she could bear. Still, she knew she had no choice. This was worse than her favourite book, *The Bells on Finland Street*. Because there was no way out, there was no happy ending, no Grandfather to come and save Elin at the end and teach her to skate on the pond. There was no pond, for heaven's sake!

Angie got up from her desk, straightened her shoulders, and went out into the kitchen, where her mom was back to poring over the bills.

"Mom?"

"Mm-hm?" asked her mother without looking up.

"Actually, I sort of lied to you earlier today."

"What?"

Angie had her mother's full attention now. She swallowed. Speak now, and there's no going back. "About practice. I said it was fine, but it wasn't. I think I'm getting worse."

"Oh, honeybun, it's hard, what you're doing. Give yourself a chance. And I don't think that quite qualifies as lying." Her mom smiled.

"No, I mean, I'm *really* getting worse. I … I think maybe I'm not enjoying it any more. It seems an awful waste of money, if I'm no good at it."

"Angel, you're not still worrying about the money? Don't even think about it — you're not a very good liar. It would kill you to stop skating. No, hon, it was a false alarm, I just figured out a way to make it work. It's all okay now."

And you're not a very good liar, either, thought Angie. "No, I'm serious, I don't want to do it any more. It's not fun, and it's too expensive, all the lessons, and ice, and dresses, and — " Angie broke off. An idea had suddenly struck her. She turned and dashed into her room. Her mom came after her.

"Don't cry, honey," she pleaded. "We'll make it okay."

"Yes," cried Angie. Maybe Grandfather couldn't save her, but Grandmother could. She went to her jewellery box and opened the lid. The little skater inside revolved slowly to the tinkling sound of "The Skater's Waltz." She took out the cheque from her grandmother and thrust it into her mother's hands. "It won't last forever, but it'll help, won't it?"

"No, Angie, Gran sent this for a dress for you. It's not for me."

"Mummy, Gran sent it so we could afford a dress. But we can't. I like my black one. Maybe we could sew an appliqué on it. They're only around twelve dollars, even the expensive ones."

"But it's not fair to you, you had your hopes up."

"Mummy, I'd rather give up the dress than quit skating altogether."

"You're my angel, you are," said Angie's mom, and she gave her a hug so hard Angie was afraid she'd squirt pea soup. She was so relieved she didn't have to stop skating that it almost didn't hurt about the dress.

5

The Zamboni Bay

Angie woke up the next morning with a mission. Today was the end of fooling around. No matter what Ginny said, she was going to win a medal and get that scholarship. It didn't have to be gold, not this year, but it had to be a medal. She had to master that axel, make it her own, never miss. She had to concentrate single-mindedly on skating. And she had to find out who had been playing tricks on Paula, if only because she wanted her win to be clean, not tainted with gossip and rumour.

Angie crunched her way through her Shredded Wheat and set off for school. She could hardly wait for lunch, to talk to Jason about how they would track down the perpetrator. She practically vibrated with impatience all the way through English and History. Who cared if she didn't have her homework done?

Naturally, she got caught, but Mr. Tibshirani didn't seem too upset with her. Most of the teachers were pretty flexible with the skaters, since there were about four of them at the school who were serious — well, five, now that Jason was here.

At five minutes to twelve, Angie hurried to the cafeteria and slid onto the bench next to Jason.

"So, okay, how are we going to look for clues?" she asked.

"Oh, so you want to be a detective now?" grinned Jason.

"I want my medal to be clean," she said with determination.

"We should go back and think about all the things that happened," said Jason. "What was the first thing?"

"The ladder," Angie replied.

"Really? The first day I came? It's a wonder people don't think it's me."

Angie quickly looked down at her carrot sticks and started fiddling with them.

"*You* thought it was me?" asked Jason. "Well, you can get off that high horse you were on when I asked if it was you."

"I didn't really think it was you. I thought for a minute it might have been, but it didn't make any sense. Anyway, I didn't know you very well then." Angie glanced sideways at Jason, and they both laughed.

"Okay, so the ladder," Jason continued. He got up from his chair, and started pacing a few feet each way. It was an odd thing to do, and it drew glances from some kids. "Sorry, I think better when I'm moving," he explained to Angie, who was also looking at him curiously. "Who was off the ice?"

"As far as I know, only me," replied Angie.

Jason looked at her sharply. "Well, then, that's why they think it's you."

"The ladder might really have been an accident. Why did Paula come off the ice early that day?"

"She said she desperately had to blow her nose."

"Oh. The ladder could have been rigged somehow. I thought of that, since no one was around. And also Paula said she thought she saw someone. The person could have been leaving the scene of the crime."

"No, I think the only explanation is you did it," teased Jason. He was still pacing agitatedly. "What was next?"

"Missing skate laces," said Angie. "That could have been anyone. Paula said she set her bag down in the hall, and there were hockey players around. Figure skaters, too, I guess."

"But in the hall, anyone could see someone taking laces."

"Too weird," replied Angie. "I can't figure that one out. Then the grape juice. I figure that was a girl, because it probably happened in the dressing room. She wouldn't leave her bag in the hall, after the laces."

"Well, that doesn't make it much easier," said Jason, shaking his head. "We need clues."

"The dress is still hanging in the change room," said Angie. "Paula never even bothered to throw it away."

"Take it, when no one's looking. Maybe it'll be a clue. But don't get caught. Then they'll think for sure it was you. Arghh!" Jason finished in exasperation, running his fingers through his coppery hair as he plonked back down in his chair.

***

After practice that night, Angie pretended she was having trouble with her skateguard to give her an excuse to stay behind and take the dress. As soon as everyone else was gone, she slipped it off the hook where it had hung for days and stuffed it quickly into her bag. She knew Paula would never miss it. Angie couldn't imagine what it could possibly tell them, but it was the closest thing to a clue that they had.

Jason was waiting for her outside in the corridor.

"Did you get it?" he asked.

"Yes, but let's not talk here. Someone might overhear," Angie replied. "Come on, I know a place." She beckoned him to follow her back into the arena.

Watching to see that they were not noticed, the pair went down the corridor to the back of the arena and slipped into the

Zamboni bay. The ice had been cleared since their practice, and a school hockey team was now warming up. Behind the hulking blue ice-resurfacer, Angie pulled the purple-stained skating dress out of her bag and held it up by the shoulders, looking at both sides.

"I don't see how we can figure out anything from this," she sighed, shaking her head. "It's not like we can dust it for fingerprints or anything."

Jason nodded, looking at the dress, then leaned with one hand against the wall, looking thoughtful.

"Oh, why bother?" snapped Angie, stuffing it back into her bag. She broke off when she saw Jason's expression change. "What?"

He was looking over the top of her head, and he slowly leaned forward and pulled something out of a pipe that was part of the arena's structure. A pair of skate laces cascaded from his hand.

Angie looked at them in surprise. "Do you think — ?"

Jason nodded. "Paula's. Bet you anything."

"But what are they doing here?"

"Well, obviously, whoever took them stashed them here. Who knows about this spot?"

"Everyone," replied Angie.

"Well, that narrows it down," was Jason's answer.

"What now?" asked Angie.

"Think there might be more clues in here?" suggested Jason. They started checking around the Zamboni and felt around the metalwork of the Zamboni bay.

"I think I see something up there," said Angie, pointing to a crevice above them. "Can you reach it?"

Even jumping on skaters' legs, Jason could not, and there was nothing they could climb on.

"Here, lift me up," said Angie, dropping her coat on her bag.

Jason put his hands on her waist. "Ready?" he asked. "One, two, three, up!"

Angie pushed off as Jason lifted her and grabbed the white corner of whatever it was. He turned her toward him as she came down, so she wouldn't land hard, just like a pairs skater would. An electrifying sensation ran through Angie. She wasn't sure if it was the excitement of possibly finding a clue, the fun of being lifted, or (no way!) the thrill of being so close to Jason.

She smiled up at him when she reached the ground, and he smiled back, holding her eyes maybe just a second longer than necessary. Angie snapped her attention away and looked at the object she had found.

"Oh, it's only an old french-fry box," she said in disgust. "Gross!" she added, as she looked inside to see congealed gravy and mold and tossed the box aside.

"Must have fallen down from the stands above here," said Jason. "I don't think it's a clue."

"Neither do I, and I don't think we're going to find anything else out here. Better put the laces back, so whoever it is doesn't know we found them. You never know."

"Right," said Jason, folding them up and stuffing them back into the pipe.

Suddenly, Angie had a thought. "You know what this means, don't you?"

"What?"

"It's definitely pranks," she said. "The ladder could have been an accident, and the laces a coincidence, if someone stole them because they wanted them. But if they stashed them here this long, they didn't want the laces, they were out to get Paula."

"You're right," said Jason.

"Well, I'd better be getting home," Angie sighed.

"I'll walk you," offered Jason. They ambled out of the arena, stopped while Jason unlocked his bicycle, and strolled down Millwood Avenue to Angie's place.

"What do we do next?" asked Angie.

"I don't know. I like to read mystery books, but I can never figure them out until they tell you at the end who did it."

"Don't they always say stuff about, what is it, motive and opportunity?" wondered Angie.

"Well, we talked about motive before. That didn't get us anywhere. So, who had opportunity?"

Angie thought about it. "Practically everybody," she finally said. "I mean, everyone's always milling around."

"I think it definitely had to be a skater," said Jason. "No adult would do silly things like that."

"Most kids wouldn't, either," Angie pointed out.

"Someone did, though. So who?"

"Probably a girl," said Angie, "since she would have more access to Paula's stuff. That kind of rules out the hockey players. Let me think. The ladder, the skate laces, the dress. The ladder is different from the others, because it attacked her, and the other things happened to her stuff. Also, it happened at the *end* of practice, and the others were at the beginning."

"Wow, Sherlock, you're good," said Jason admiringly. "Next you'll be telling me what brand of baby powder the culprit uses, and what they had for breakfast."

"Yeah, but what does it mean?"

"Well, what if the ladder *is* different?" Jason suggested. "What if it's not related?"

"Yeah?"

"Then we're looking for someone who sabotages Paula's stuff just before practice. Why?"

"Cuts into practice time," said Angie matter-of-factly.

"So it must be somebody who wants her to do badly. That cuts out the hockey players. What are people usually doing before practice?"

"Watching the hockey players," said Angie. "Another reason it's not one of them. In fact, why were there hockey players near the canteen thc day the laces disappeared? They should have been playing."

"Does everyone watch hockey?"

Angie looked at Jason. They had arrived at Angie's place and were standing talking at the bottom of the stairs. "I don't know."

"Then that's what we do next. Watch who's watching hockey. And the players, too."

Angie shivered. "I'd better go in," she said. "Mom's probably got dinner ready."

"Okay," Jason replied. "Tomorrow, we watch."

"See ya," said Angie, clanging up the stairs to the back porch and into the apartment.

***

Next day, Angie beetled as fast as she could from school over to the arena. When she arrived, she glanced in at the rink, but none of the other figure skaters was there. She decided she would get into her skates and go out and watch. No skaters were in the dressing room, either, though a couple of younger girls came in while she was lacing on her skates. Angie said hi to them and then went out and climbed into the stands.

The Hornets were playing against each other in a mock game. Angie watched the players whiz around the rink. Even at a distance, the guys seemed enormous. Like a lot of figure skaters, Angie was small for her age and compact in build. But most of the hockey players were big and beefy, and even the ones who weren't looked that way because of all the padding they had on. Some of the girls thought certain ones were cute, and she had to admit that there was something about Kevin Bessey that she found appealing, but the rest were just like big snarly bears lumbering around on skates.

It wasn't long before other skaters joined her in the stands. Jennifer, Paula, and Tiiu sat together near the front. She saw Jason come in a little while later, but he headed straight for the change room. Good idea. They didn't want to be obvious about their spying.

The Hornets were playing well, and Angie was enjoying watching them. Even if she wasn't that crazy about the players, she did like hockey — the sharp whistles, the echoing shouts, and especially the clack of the sticks against each other as the players scrabbled for the puck in the corners.

Kevin tipped in a particularly pretty goal, and the spectators clapped. Just then the honking buzzer went off, signalling the end of the Hornets' ice time. The Zamboni began chugging out of its bay, and Angie glanced over to see Paula and Tiiu moving toward the change room. Jennifer was nowhere to be seen.

6

Angie the Spy

Angie could have kicked herself for not watching to see when Jennifer left or where she went. Chances were that she had gone to the dressing room to put on her skates, so even though Angie already had her skates on, she went to check there first.

No Jennifer.

Just in case, Angie waited a moment to see if she would emerge from the washroom, but she was anxious to get out on the ice and finally left without seeing her.

Angie was warming up when Jennifer finally appeared, looking slightly breathless. But Paula was already stroking around the arena, so apparently nothing had happened to her that day to make her late ... unless Jennifer had been up to something else, something that would happen after practice. Something that made Jennifer late — which was kind of unlike her. She was a really dedicated skater. Angie didn't know her all that well, since Jennifer was a year older, and never really had the time of day for anyone outside of her "crowd."

Angie could hardly concentrate on her skating. In fact, she couldn't concentrate at all. The only axel she landed clean was horribly ungainly, and even her spins, usually her best (and favourite) element, were off. She couldn't seem to find her centre today. It was all a question of balance, and she didn't have any.

"You've got to hold that centre from inside your very heart," exhorted Ginny. "Remember that tight wire running right through the top of your head!"

A few minutes later, it was, "Angie, Angie, what are you doing with your hands? You look like a rag doll! And where are your shoulders? Where's your head?"

Where *is* my head, thought Angie. Thinking about those stupid pranks, when I should be thinking about skating. Come on Angie! Practice, practice, and more practice, but concentrate!

Afterwards, Angie had hoped Jason would walk home with her again, but she saw that he and Paula were deep in conversation with Céline and Bob — at least Bob and Jason were. Céline was looking daggers at Paula, and Paula was looking everywhere but at her mother.

It didn't seem worth waiting around, so Angie trudged off in the snow by herself. It was cold, and the snow squeaked as she walked. Why did life have to get so complicated? If only she could concentrate on one thing — her skating. Everything else was taking up too much of her energy, and she was never going to master a double axel if she couldn't even do her spins. School, home, skating, money — as if all that wasn't enough, why did she have to get involved in this stupid detective case?

As Angie rolled around in bed that night trying to sleep (no problem spinning now, Angie!), she tried to visualize her perfect program. Besides lulling her to sleep and helping her skate better, the best part was that it sometimes led to dreaming about skating in a way that no one on earth could really skate. When she dreamed of skating, the ice had no friction and she would glide effortlessly through each element. Sometimes, in a spin, she would spin so many times that she lost count of the turns, eighteen, nineteen, twenty, forty, sixty, a hundred revolutions. The crowd was cheering and rising to its feet as she spun on and on, not getting tired, not feeling dizzy, not feeling any muscle soreness as she held her leg perfectly pointed in front of her, changing positions and feet two or three times, finally moving into the Biellmann spin, raising her leg high over her head and grasping the blade of her skate with no effort at all.

That was if she could manage a dream like that. Tonight, her bedcovers felt like a net that had been thrown over her and her blades and her fingers kept getting caught on the cords as she tangled herself up worse than ever.

***

The next day at lunch, Angie found Jason at their usual table.

"So," Jason asked eagerly, "did you find out anything?"

"Jennifer left before the end of hockey practice, but I didn't see her go, so I couldn't follow her," said Angie ruefully.

"Rats. But that's interesting," said Jason.

"Yeah, and she wasn't in the change room when I went there, and she was late for practice."

"That's *really* interesting," replied Jason.

"But nothing happened. At least, did it? Did anything happen after? I saw you guys talking."

"Not that I know of," said Jason. "We stayed about half an hour. I think everyone else was gone by the time Paula and I left. Nothing happened by then."

"So, dead end," Angie said.

"Yeah."

"That's all there seems to be," she moaned.

"Yeah."

"I don't know what to do."

"I guess we've got to keep watching everything," said Jason, "until whoever it is strikes again."

Angie sighed.

***

The next day, the scene repeated itself: hockey practice, Angie arriving early, Tiiu, Paula, and Jennifer watching the players. This time, though, Angie was determined not to let Jennifer get away if she slipped out. And again, just before the whistle, Jennifer left the stands. Angie got up to follow her, trying to look casual.

To Angie's surprise, Jennifer went straight into the ladies' change room. Angie followed her in, and headed for her own equipment bag, watching Jennifer out of the corner of her eye. Jennifer opened her bag and pulled out her skates; she was already dressed for practice otherwise. In order to look busy, Angie rummaged around in her bag, grabbed a chapstick, and began to run it over her lips. Then, carrying her skates and in stocking feet, Jennifer hurried out of the room.

Waiting a moment, so as not to make Jennifer suspicious, Angie emerged from the dressing room. Although Jennifer had only left a few seconds before, she was nowhere to be seen. Angie checked the stands in the arena, but only Paula and Tiiu were there, gathering up their stuff to go to the dressing room themselves. Next, she looked down each of the corridors, but she didn't see Jennifer anywhere. It was nearly time to go onto the ice, so Angie gave up.

Frustration, frustration. How was she ever going to solve this mystery? As she warmed up, Angie fairly attacked the ice. Paula came on, sporting an enormous hole in her tights and an indignant air.

"Look at this," she exclaimed to Tiiu. "Look at this hole! What next?"

Well, now. A hole in Paula's tights. It had to have happened sometime between last night and today's practice.

Could Jennifer possibly have had enough time to tear Paula's tights in the few seconds she was in the change room before Angie came in? As pranks went, it was fairly lame. It hadn't made Paula more than a few moments late for practice. Maybe it was meant to upset her, or it was revenge for something. As Angie glided over to greet Ginny, Tiiu stroked past and gave Angie a hostile stare. Jennifer had just stepped onto the ice, with the same breathless look as yesterday — not really breathless, just kind of pink and lively.

Today, the axel was fairly good, but the spins were lost altogether. Spins, which she had been a natural at ever since she was tiny. She wobbled, her skate tracing left a huge circle, she even fell once. And her footwork!

"Take it easy, Ange," called Ginny from the sidelines. "You look like you're trying to chop onions with your skates. You're the Princess Bride, not a handi-chop! Light! Light! Light!"

When practice came to an end, Ginny called her over.

"What's going on?" she asked. "You're all over the place. There's all kinds of fire, but no control."

"Nothing's going on," said Angie. "I guess I'm just not concentrating. I'll do better, I promise."

"It's the scholarship, isn't it?" demanded Ginny. "I told you, don't worry about it this year. You just have to do your best. I've told you before, you don't just come in cold and get medals. You have to work your way up. It's just the way judging is. If they don't know you, they have to leave room above you for the skaters they know will skate well. And then if you turn out to be better, they can't give the big skaters low marks or they look bad. You've got to earn your stripes. And skating erratically like this, who knows how you'll skate on the day? You've simply *got* to focus."

Angie looked down and chipped the ice slightly with her toe pick. Ginny was always — well not *always* calm — but always sensible.

"I'm sorry Ginny, really. Honestly, I'll do better tomorrow."

**

At lunch the next day, Angie brought Jason up to date on the latest developments. Of course, he knew about the hole in the stocking. There was hardly anyone in the northern hemisphere who didn't, but he was intrigued by Jennifer's strange behaviour.

"It's got to be Jennifer," said Jason. "She must be feeling threatened by Paula."

"But she couldn't have had time to open Paula's bag, tear the tights, put them back and get to her bag by the time I came in," Angie pointed out.

"Maybe she did it at another time."

"Yeah, but that makes no sense. First, Paula would have been wearing them when Jennifer left yesterday. Second, why did Jennifer go into the change room? And then where did she go? And why would she tear the tights anyway? It doesn't make sense. Besides, I'm pretty sure Paula had her bag with her in the stands today. I mean, would you leave your bag around after all that's happened to her?"

"Paula must have more than one pair of tights. Maybe it happened yesterday after practice, to another pair," suggested Jason.

"Then it could have been anyone. And we're back to square one."

"See if Jennifer leaves at the end of hockey practice again tomorrow. Try not to lose her this time."

**

On day three, the scenario was the same: hockey practice, Angie arriving early, Tiiu, Paula, and Jennifer watching the players. This time, though, Angie was sitting on the end of the stands, where she could see the door to the change room. This time, when Jennifer slipped out, Angie let her go. Sure enough, Jennifer went to the change room. A few moments later she came out, in stocking feet, carrying her skates, like yesterday. She turned right, past the wall of photos, and then went left, down the north corridor under the stands. Angie stepped out of the stands, trying to keep Jennifer in sight. Jennifer hurried down the corridor and then turned left again, toward the Zamboni bay — the Zamboni bay where the skate laces had been stashed!

Angie moved down the corridor as quietly as she could, on the toes of her skateguards. She heard the buzzer that ended the hockey practice, and soon the Zamboni chugged out onto the ice surface. Quietly moving closer to the bay, which she couldn't see into from this angle, she thought she heard low voices. So, Jennifer had an accomplice! No wonder it was impossible to pin anything on her. Then silence. Angie tried to move to an angle where she could see and not be seen, but it was difficult to know where that would be. She could just make out the edge of Jennifer's red skirt, and something black and orange — a Hornets sweater? Angie leaned a little farther out — and quickly pulled back. Jennifer was there all right. Angie knew her red skirt and the black sweater with the zigzags and her beautiful black hair. And she also recognized the Hornets uniform, and Kevin Bessey's longish blond hair, even though she could see neither of their faces, because they were stuck together in a kryptonite lip lock.

7

The Missing Skates

Whether Kevin heard something or whether his Gretzky-like peripheral vision worked even when his eyes were closed, he knew Angie was there.

"Hey!" he called out.

Blushing, Angie stepped from behind the wall.

"Little sneak!" exclaimed Jennifer. "What are you doing, following me?"

"No, um, I — " Angie couldn't think of any reason on earth why she would logically be back there, unless she had been following Jennifer, which, of course, she had been. "Sorry," she finished up lamely.

Kevin said nothing, just wiped his mouth on the sleeve of his sweater.

But Jennifer said plenty. "You brat. Don't you ever dare tell anyone you saw me here, or I'll kill you. I'll … I'll … I know you're the one who's been playing tricks on Paula, and I'll tell. I've got proof."

Angie blinked. How could Jennifer have proof of something that hadn't happened?

"Um, Jennifer," interrupted Kevin. "The Zamboni." He jerked his head toward the machine that was finishing up its rounds.

"Get out of here," Jennifer shot at Angie.

Angie was only too glad to go. As she walked away, she heard Kevin saying, "See you tomorrow? Same time, same place?"

"Are you kidding?" snapped Jennifer. "Now that the little brat knows? You know my parents would have a fit …"

Anyway, Angie didn't care about that. She was much more puzzled by Jennifer's strange accusation. How, she asked herself again, could Jennifer have proof that Angie was behind the pranks when she wasn't? Did that mean that Jennifer was really the culprit, and that she planned to pin it on Angie? But why would she do that?

Or did it mean that Jennifer just assumed that it was Angie and made up the bit about there being proof to scare her into silence? Or was Jennifer just grasping at straws? There were only two possible explanations. Either Jennifer was behind the pranks, or she didn't know who was.

Angie didn't have much time to come up with answers. When she emerged from the hallway under the stands, she found the corridor in pandemonium.

Paula, as Angie quickly figured out, was at the centre of whatever it was. Nothing new about that. But this time, she was panicky and nearly in tears. Her mom was quizzing her, and the rest of the girls were standing around with eyes like saucers.

"Are you sure you had them with you?" Céline was asking her daughter.

Paula's voice showed her distress. "Yes! I told you! I'm sure!"

"What's going on?" Angie whispered to Tiiu. Tiiu just gave her a chilly look and turned her ice-blond head away.

One of the little girls filled her in. "Paula's skates are missing."

Her skates! This was serious. Not long ago, Paula had got a new pair of skates — Riedell Goldstars with Wilson blades.

They must have cost over five hundred dollars. They might not be the most expensive skates you could get, but they were still very good skates.

"Someone must have stolen them," cried Paula. "I think we should check everyone's stuff!"

"Now, now," said Céline. "We can't go accusing people of things right away. Let's search around the arena."

"By that time the thief will have escaped!"

Really, thought Angie, this was quite the scene, even from an attention-grabber like Paula. Obviously Céline thought so too.

"Paula!" she said sharply. "We don't go calling people thieves. We look around the arena first."

"I'll help you," said Tiiu.

Angie hoped there wouldn't be a wholesale move to help with Paula's search. Maybe Paula could afford to miss a practice, since her parents were her coaches, but ice time was rented and Ginny was being paid, and Angie couldn't afford to waste the money or the time. Besides, what had Paula ever done for her? But she knew that if everyone volunteered, she'd have to as well or she'd just look mean — and guilty, too. And what if she were the one to find the skates? Then Jennifer and Tiiu and Paula would assume that she knew where they were all along. Luckily, Céline took charge.

"No, you and I will look while everyone else goes to practice right now. Jason, you go and warm up, at least." As the group dispersed, Angie heard Paula's mom begin a lecture about carelessness, and she was glad she wasn't on the receiving end. It was true, though. Paula was stunningly careless with her things. It made Angie kind of mad that Paula took her stuff so much for granted that she left it lying around, while Angie always had to squeak just one more practice out of old skates and clothes.

Jennifer's comments and Paula's soap opera didn't do much for Angie's concentration, and she had a bad practice the second day in a row. Angie knew that she was going to have to give herself a good talking to later on. She couldn't let this nonsense get to her and undermine what she knew she could really do.

After practice, the skates still weren't found, and Dave called all the skaters together.

"You all know what's happened," he told them. "And I understand that a few other little incidents have been happening around here. I have three things to tell you. Most important — this *will not* be tolerated. Second, if anyone knows anything, I want to know it. No one will know who told. Third, don't leave your stuff lying around until we find out what's going on."

"Finally," Dave continued, after a pause to let his words sink in. "As I said, this will not be tolerated. We *will* find out what's going on, and if any of the skaters is involved, you will be suspended *permanently* from the club." Dave turned and walked off briskly. Angie had never seen him so angry. The skaters stood numbed for a moment before they quietly drifted into the dressing rooms to get ready to go home. Paula was surrounded by her usual gang, and Angie heard Paula say in a shaky voice that her mom thought the insurance might cover the missing skates. She looked like she might have been crying, or almost crying. Despite her annoyance at Paula, she did feel a tiny twinge of pity. Imagine losing a pair of Goldstars with Wilson blades.

Just then a knock came at the dressing room door. Jason's voice called out, "Everybody decent?"

"Yes!" the younger girls chorused.

Jason stuck his head around the door, smiling. "Look what I found outside," he said, as his arm emerged from behind the door, holding a pair of white skates. "These belong to anyone?" he teased.

"My skates!" shrieked Paula as she ran forward to take them. "Where did you find them?"

"I was unlocking my bike, and when I bent down to take the lock off, I saw something white under a bush. I thought it was probably a plastic bag or something, but I decided to check it out, and there they were." Angie saw Jason glance at her. She looked around. Did anyone look guilty, or surprised, or angry, or relieved? Well, actually everyone looked relieved, except Tiiu, who looked kind of angry.

"Oh, what a scare!" sighed Paula. "Thank you, Jason, thank you, thank you."

Jason ducked back out of the dressing room, and Paula, with Jennifer and Tiiu in her wake, rushed out with the skates to tell Céline the good news.

When Angie had changed and emerged from the dressing room, she saw Tiiu waiting by the corridor under the stands. As usual, her white-blonde hair was scraped back off her face into a tight bun, and her eyes and nose both looked sharp. When she saw Angie, she signalled her to come over. A little apprehensively, Angie went.

"Come back here," said Tiiu, pulling Angie out of sight of the front corridor.

Angie was getting more and more nervous. What was going on?

"Look, we all know it's you who's doing all that stuff to Paula. So quit it."

"Me?" spluttered Angie. "I never did anything!"

"Oh yeah?" challenged Tiiu, holding up a fist. She extended her fingers one by one as she enumerated her evidence. "One. You were the only person off the ice when the ladder fell. Two. Jennifer found Paula's laces in the Zamboni bay, and she says you like to snoop around back there. Three.

You dumped the grape juice because you're jealous. Four.
Where were you before practice today? Stealing her skates,
which I say is just plain criminal. Did you think Paula
wouldn't recognize them when you showed up wearing them?
Five. This all started the day Jason got here. You're trying to
wreck her skating so thcy'll partner him with you. I've seen
how you two are all lovey-dovey and hanging out together all
the time. And if you do one more thing, I'm telling Dave. So
quit it. Or they'll throw you out of the club."

Angie's mouth fell open. If she didn't know better, she'd
believe she'd done it too. Then slowly she began to feel angry.
She had never done a thing to Paula. It wasn't fair that everyone suspected her.

"That is absolutely untrue!" she said, her voice shaking.

"As far as I'm concerned, you're guilty until proven inno-
cent," said Tiiu spitefully. "Which will be never."

Angie was aghast. She knew Tiiu was wrong, but how
could she ever prove it? "I don't have to stand here and take
this," she finally answered and turned on her heel and walked
away. She felt the dozens of eyes from the wall of photos
which seemed to follow her as she went.

Angie stepped out of the arena into a biting wind that
blew tiny, hard pellets of snow into her face. It had been
snowing steadily all day, and as she trudged through the
drifts, some of it spilled into her short boots and melted there,
making Angie even more miserable than she already was, if
that were possible.

She was never going to be able to solve this mystery, so
why even try? Every time she and Jason thought they had a
lead, it crumbled to nothing. It seemed like it wasn't Jennifer.
How could she have hid the skates *and* met Kevin in the
Zamboni bay? Could it be Tiiu? That was a possibility. Or
someone else, someone she hadn't thought of yet? One of the

younger girls? A boy? *Could* it be Jason? No, the only logical culprit Angie had heard of so far was Angie.

And then there was still the money problem. The cheque from her grandmother helped, but it didn't solve everything. And that led her to thinking about the competition. Could she get a scholarship? Yikes! It was only a week away! And she still hadn't mastered the double axel, and all her other elements were eroding at the same time.

The snow was starting to let up, and as Angie looked up at the sky, the clouds were breaking up a little. A star shone through and Angie stopped and looked at it. Maybe she was a little old for it, but it was time to make a wish.

"Star light, star bright," she murmured. "First star I see tonight. Wish I may, wish I might, have the wish I wish tonight." Then she scrunched up her eyes and tried to decide what was the best thing to wish for.

"I wish I had a beautiful dress for the competition," she suddenly whispered.

How odd it seemed to Angie that she had wished for a dress, not money, or the axel, or winning the scholarship, or solving the mystery. A dress. Because if she had a dress, a beautiful dress, she would feel like the Princess Bride, and she would land the axel, and win the scholarship. Maybe she could even, like Sara Crewe in *A Little Princess*, rise above Tiiu and Jennifer's mean accusations. *That* was who she had to be, not the Princess Bride, but the Little Princess, who rose above poverty, and unkindness, and greed, and in the end, she won.

The wind seemed a little less harsh as Angie turned the corner and climbed the metal steps to her apartment.

8

Dying for a Dress

"Got much homework tonight, angel?" Angie's mom asked her over dinner.

"No, we just have to do some questions for Math, that's all."

"Good, because I happened to glance into your room today, and I think it's about time you tidied it up."

"Aw, Mom," moaned Angie, even though she knew her mother was right. She just wasn't a neat kind of person. She'd always throw her dirty clothes into the basket in the corner, but the clean ones were usually piled in heaps on her dresser, chair, and floor. And she never, ever left dirty dishes or empty pop cans in the room, but books, magazines, hair thingies, shoes, jewellery, school stuff, and skating stuff were strewn about the place. She was forever losing earrings, but she always found them again eventually.

Once the dishes and her homework were done, Angie heaved a huge sigh, and began to sort out the stuff. The only way she could face the task was by making a game of it. Sometimes she'd be systematic, like starting at the door and working her way counterclockwise around the room, or starting from the highest surface and working her way down. Or she'd do something really inefficient, like trying to find everything in the room that belonged in the closet and putting it there, and then working on everything that belonged on her desk and so on. Today, she decided to work by colour, starting with everything that was red.

A sweater, a hair scrunchee, a book. She thought again about Tiiu's accusation today. Everything blue. A pair of tights, another book, a teddy bear, gloves. Obviously, Tiiu was the one who was playing the tricks. She worked her way through green (Tiiu had figured everything out to keep the blame off herself), black (but why on earth would she want to harm Paula?), and brown (maybe there was something going on that Angie didn't know about), and was working on white when she came upon Paula's ruined skating dress.

She shook it out and held it up in front of her. It really was ruined, the purple stain splashed right over the front and sleeve. She thought of Sara Crewe again, in her patched black mourning dress, still being able to rise above all the unkindness and unfairness that was thrown at her. Angie would be wearing just an old black dress to the competition. But just as she couldn't be Elin from *The Bells on Finland Street*, saved by Grandfather, no Indian Gentleman with a monkey would be moving in next door any time soon. Anyway, she didn't live in an attic, and she didn't have a skylight. But maybe she could still be a princess, if she believed hard enough.

Right now, though, Angie just couldn't. Somehow, thinking about everything just made her depressed again. She couldn't believe in anything. No wishing on stars, no lucky charms could help her, and it was all too much to try to do by herself. She'd never land the double axel, she'd never solve the mystery, she'd never skate in a beautiful midnight blue dress with rhinestones and a double skirt that was white underneath.

Angie flopped down on the bed, clutching Paula's dress, and started to cry. When her mother came in and turned out the light and pulled the blanket over her, Angie was so sound asleep that she never even felt it.

***

When Angie woke up the next morning, she couldn't remember at first why she was still in her clothes. She remembered she'd been thinking about dresses and found she was still clutching Paula's old white one, partly dyed purple.

And that was when the idea came to her. Dark blue dye would easily cover the white, and likely the purple, on the dress. The black trim would stay black, but from a distance the judges would never notice. Even up close, people would probably think it was just a different fabric, or a trick of the light. She bounced out of bed. It was Saturday.

***

At the rink, Angie was lacing up her skates when Paula came in, followed closely by Céline.

"Sit down over here," Céline was saying. "Let's have a look." Gently, she unzipped Paula's boot and slowly worked it off her foot, to the chorus of "oohs" and "ows" that bubbled from Paula.

"What happened?" asked Jennifer.

"Somebody — ow! — pushed me down on the ice outside," reported Paula. "A guy rode by on a bike."

Jason?

"Did you see who it was?" asked Tiiu.

"No. Ouch, Mom! He went too fast."

Céline was examining Paula's foot. "I'm not so sure he pushed you. Are you sure you didn't just slip? Maybe he startled you?"

"Didn't you *see*?" moaned Paula.

"No, I didn't see. I was talking to your father."

Tiiu and Jennifer glanced at each other, and then at Angie. This was too much! Did they think she'd been in two places at once?

"Well, let's take you to emergency if it's that bad, poor little thing," said Céline, stroking her daughter's head. Paula started to cry. "I'll get your papa."

As soon as the girls were alone in the dressing room, Tiiu turned to Angie. "I told you to leave her alone! I'm telling."

"Don't be ridiculous," said Angie. "How could I push her? I was in here with you!"

Jennifer and Tiiu looked at each other. Clearly, they were stumped. Paula whimpered softly in the corner, and Jennifer sat down and took her hand.

"She got somebody to do it, like that American skater, remember?" Clearly, Tiiu was not willing to be diverted from her suspicions.

"Give me a break," snapped Angie. "Thirteen-year-olds do not hire hit men. I've had as much as I'm going to take of this."

As she turned and left the change room, Angie could hear Tiiu behind her. "Do you notice? Each thing that happens gets worse and worse. I wonder what that brat has up her sleeve next."

Just before the door swung shut and cut off the conversation, Jennifer said, "We'd better watch out for you at Skate Scarborough ... "

Once she was out on the ice, Angie tried to put all the unpleasantness behind her. She had not worn her usual, kind of old, practice clothes today. She was dressed in her simple black dress, with black leggings. She had wanted to feel elegant, special-looking. She wanted to remember to be a princess. She was glad she had.

Sara Crewe — or rather Angie — began stroking around the surface. She did some backward skating, testing out her edges and spins a little. She let the wind rush past her and blow away all the nonsense of the past weeks. Soon, warming up, she peeled off her sweatshirt, and was tossing it into the penalty box when Ginny arrived.

"Angie, what are you doing in costume?" Ginny asked.

"Skate Scarborough is a week from today," said Angie. "I need a dress rehearsal."

"Okay," said Ginny doubtfully. "But I want to see pretty skating, not just nice clothes. Let's do a run-through."

Angie just smiled to herself, as Ginny went to put *The Princess Bride* music on the system. It was the convention that whoever's music was playing had the right of way, so she just shut out the other skaters and began to skate. Her second jump, about half a minute into the music, was the double axel. Ginny thought it was best to have a chance to get over the jitters before the jump, but then to get the double axel over with as soon as possible, leaving her two and a half minutes to get back on track if necessary. The opening began with the spiral, then a few uncomplicated bits of gliding and footwork, and a simple jump, nothing fancy, with a camel spin changing to a sit spin at about the middle of that section.

Then, skating forward on the left outside edge of her blade, in a curving arc, she pushed off hard with her left foot, bringing her arms in as she spun counterclockwise, landing on her right foot, still curving in a counterclockwise direction, and landing a perfect — *single* — axel. Never mind now, thought Angie, just keep going. A nicely centred layback spin, a *really* deep spreadeagle, a few simpler jumps, and the final, balletic backward footwork and slide to close the program.

"Okay," said Ginny. "Pretty good, except for the double axel. The single was nicely done, but the top skaters at this level have the double, so you're going to have to work on it. What happened?"

"I couldn't pull it off," said Angie. "I just knew I didn't have the snap going up."

"We need to work on your costume, too, I'm afraid. It was fine for your Alley Cat number last year, but all black isn't very princessy." She tugged at Angie's sleeve. "Anyway, you're starting to grow out of it."

"My mom said I could sew on some appliqués," said Angie. She didn't want to give away her idea about dyeing the old white dress just yet — what if it didn't work?

"Okay, that sounds good," said Ginny. "Now, go and practise your axel. Your *double* axel."

While others took turns with their music, Angie practised the double axel over and over. Practice, practice, and more practice. By the end of the session, it really was getting better — she landed a few very nice ones — and even if it was still inconsistent, there was a chance she might get it at the competition.

***

The crowds were starting to collect for the afternoon public skating, and Angie could smell the oil for the fries heating up and the wet-wool smell that seemed to hover around the kids who came to skate. Boys came clattering into the stands, shoving each other and kicking the boards. Girls with department-store skates and no skateguards on whispered and giggled as they waited for their turn to go on the ice. It was time to go.

Angie wanted to stop and talk to Jason, to tell him about the latest developments but she didn't see him around anywhere.

Two boys a little younger than Angie were looking at the big picture of Bob and Céline just outside the snack bar.

"Look at the sissy figure skater," said one.

"I don't know. Could you lift a girl up over your head?"
replied the other.

The first one looked at his friend. "Who would want to?"
Both boys snickered and dashed onto the ice.

Angie just rolled her eyes. It was typical, but it was too
bad some kids couldn't see what a tough sport figure skating
really was.

She didn't have time to look for Jason. She had important
stuff to do.

***

Late in the afternoon, Angie checked on the dress, hanging
over the shower rail next to a couple of pairs of her mom's
pantyhose. It was dry. The place where the trim had been
black was definitely darker than the rest, but it couldn't be
helped. The grape stain could be made out only if you looked
really closely. The underskirt and bottom of the dress were
still pure white. Wrapping that part in a plastic bag and holding it out of the sink had worked. There was a slight blurriness
where it joined, but no one would ever see that in a spin. The
only problem was that the sink in the tiny bathroom now had
a blueish cast, even after Angie had scrubbed it with cleanser.
Angie hoped her mother wouldn't be cross, but since nothing
co-ordinated in the bathroom anyway, she probably wouldn't
care.

Finally, Angie took a piece of chalk and marked where she
wanted her "rhinestones." She had looked at sew-on rhinestones, but even the cheap ones were expensive. Well, if Sara
Crewe could imagine white handkerchiefs into gold plates,
she could imagine sequins and beads into diamonds.

She sewed each "diamond" on individually and knotted it
carefully on the inside. It was considered very bad form to
lose bits of your costume on the ice. If you didn't trip on

them, other people might. The needle through the chalk mark, then a silver sequin for reflection, then a plastic crystal bead from an old necklace of her mom's, then a tiny, clear glass bead to hold it on, and back through.

At last, she tried on her new costume. She was looking critically at herself in the mirror when her mom came in from grocery shopping.

"Oh, princess," she said when she saw Angie. "Wherever did you get such a beautiful dress?"

9

The Culprit ...

Skate Scarborough was being held at the Galaxy this year. Angie had heard about this wonderful, scary rink, but had never been there before. She found out just why it was so wonderful and scary as soon as she arrived and checked in. It wasn't a hockey rink. It was a figure-skating rink. There were no boards, no penalty box. Stands were along one side and one end, with the judges on the other side and a wall painted with green and blue swirls at the other end. Angie started to get nervous. Without any boards, how would she know where she was?

The first thing she did was check the schedule, so she could let her mom know more or less when she was skating. It wouldn't be until two o'clock. She dashed out to the car to tell her.

"I'll be here, honey," said her mom before driving off.

Back inside, she found Ginny, and she saw Jennifer, Paula, and Tiiu checking the schedule. Ginny coached a couple of skaters from another rink who were skating earlier in a different category, so Angie decided to watch them while she waited for her turn. She didn't want to get into her new costume too soon, because she was afraid Paula or someone else might recognize it and say something that would upset her.

As she watched the skaters go through their paces, she thought back over the week. She had finally managed to talk to Jason at lunch on Monday and had told him about Jennifer making out with Kevin Bessey and then about Tiiu accusing her of being the mischief-maker. Jason filled Angie in on Paula. Apparently, Paula had merely twisted her ankle; it wasn't broken or even sprained. Everyone had been worried that she might have to miss Skate Scarborough, but it seemed she would be able to compete, although she'd certainly missed some much-needed practice time. Jason had been keen to develop theories (Was she pushed? Did she fall?) and to do more sleuthing, but somehow, Angie's heart had gone out of the whole thing. To her, it just felt tedious now, not the fun adventure it had seemed at first. After all, she was a skater, not a detective, and if she didn't put her whole concentration into her program, what was the point in solving mysteries? She didn't want to be Nancy Drew any more, she wanted to be Elizabeth Manley. And she certainly didn't want to think about what would happen if anything else befell Paula, and Tiiu decided she was going to turn Angie in.

Then, Monday after school, she had been anxious to show Ginny her new costume.

"I have a surprise for you after practice," she had told her coach.

"So do I," Ginny had replied.

After practice, Angie had dawdled until Tiiu and Jennifer were gone, to show Ginny the dress. As soon as she saw it, Ginny had started to laugh.

"It's gorgeous!" she said, and then pulled a paper bag out of her duffel bag.

Angie opened it. Inside were three long pieces of fine white tulle, bunched up in ruffles.

"I thought your black dress needed a little more romance. I thought you could put these around the cuffs and neck. But I guess you don't really need them."

Angie laid the tulle around the neckline of the dark blue dress. "But they're perfect!" she exclaimed. "They hide the old black trim."

"You're right," agreed Ginny.

The tulle sewed onto the sleeves and neckline had made the whole dress into a fantasy. Angie's mom had bought the shimmery tights, too. And later on, Gran and Pop were coming, and her mom, and Angie was going to skate in this strange arena with an on-again, off-again double axel and Yikes.

Ginny climbed up and sat next to her. "One of my other girls is in the next flight," she told Angie. A flight was a group of skaters. Usually there were so many skaters in each category that they had to be divided into flights, or the judges couldn't possibly evaluate them. There were four flights for Angie's category, and the top three from each would go on to compete in the finals tomorrow.

"How are you doing?" Ginny was asking her.

"Okay," Angie said. "This is an unusual rink."

"I think you'll like skating in it — without the boards, there's a sense of freedom."

"I'm worried I'll skate right off the ice and trip."

"You'll be fine if you stick to the choreography. Just be careful coming out of the layback spin. You're near the middle of the ice, so remember to go toward the blue and green wall, not toward the end stands, or you'll end up skating the rest of the program in the wrong end of the rink."

Oh great, one more thing to worry about.

"I brought you a little present," said Ginny. "For luck." She gave Angie a little bag with tissue tucked into it. Angie opened it up.

"It's for your hair," said Ginny.

It was a little row of pink satin rosebuds with trailing white ribbons to decorate her tied-back hair.

"It's beautiful," said Angie, her eyes sparkling. "Thank you!"

"Time for you to start thinking of getting dressed. Go on," Ginny told her.

In the dressing room, Angie found a quiet corner to get changed in and to go over her routine in her mind. She always liked to visualize a perfect performance before anything important, just as she often put herself to sleep at night skating through the program in her head. She pulled on her shimmery tights, and then, a little nervously, her midnight blue dress with "diamonds" and frothy trim. She brushed her light brown hair back, tied her new rosebud hair ornament on, and pinned the ends under with bobby pins. Finally, she laced up her skates, two hooks at a time, for luck. Then, she sat quietly in the corner of the deserted change room with her eyes closed and started the music of *The Princess Bride* in her mind.

The door creaked open and banged shut, and Angie glanced over to see who was there. It was Paula. She crossed the dressing room and went into the washroom with her garment bag and skates, without even noticing Angie. A few minutes later, Paula came back, hung up her bag and left the room, either not seeing Angie or ignoring her as usual.

The dressing room was starting to get busier, as skaters came in to check their costumes one last time, and one flight finished skating.

"Did you see how bad my camel spin was?" one girl asked.

"It was fine, quit worrying," her friend answered.

Angie continued visualizing. Perfect spins, dead on centre. Clean, explosive jumps that almost hung in mid-air. Footwork like Ginger Rogers.

Soon, Paula came in with Tiiu and Jennifer, chatting. "I'm glad I'm not in the same flight as you guys," Tiiu was saying. "At least I can get beaten by strangers."

Paula was unzipping her garment bag. Suddenly she gasped.

"Oh my gosh!" gulped Tiiu. Angie looked over.

At first she couldn't see what had happened, but then Paula took her dress right out of the bag. It was a gorgeous, dramatic red dress, with black lace over the bodice. And the bodice had a jagged, frayed tear right down the middle. In the silence that followed, Jennifer and Tiiu slowly turned to look at Angie.

Angie got up to leave the room. She didn't care if it made her look guilty. She knew she wasn't. She couldn't afford to let this latest development unbalance her. She just didn't dare think of what Dave might say when Tiiu accused her. Wasn't it just her luck to be alone in the change room with the dress? As she passed the stony stares of the Millwood skaters, she lowered her eyes. Well, that probably made her look guilty, too. She noticed a thread caught on one of Paula's skateguards.

I hope she steps on it and trips, Angie thought for a moment, but she quickly pushed the spiteful thought away. She was the princess. She was above it all. Spite wasn't worthy of her. She raised her head proudly and left the room, climbing into the stands away from other people to finish her visualization.

"Hey, mind if I join you?" came a familiar voice.

"Hi, Jason, come on up," she said. Since it was almost time for her to skate, there was nothing more she could do.

"You look terrific," said Jason. "New dress?"

Angie smiled sheepishly. "Very old dress," she admitted. "Can't you detect the grape-juice stain?" She showed him the faint line that marked the edge of it.

Jason's mouth dropped open, and then he grinned.

Down at the other end of the rink, some of the little girls from the Millwood Club were gathered to cheer for the Millwood skaters. Paula was the only one in the next flight from the club. In fact, each of the four of them at their level was in a different flight.

"Paula, Paula, do your best," they were chanting. "Even if you *don't*, you've got the *prettiest dress*!"

"Not anymore," said Angie to Jason.

"What do you mean?"

"Somebody tore it. I mean, really sliced ... it ... Jason!"

"What?"

"It's Paula!

"What's Paula?"

"Paula's being doing all that stuff to herself!"

"What? Why?"

"There was a red thread on her skateguard," Angie went on. "Her dress is the same red. Paula must have cut the dress with her skate when she went to the washroom."

"But why?"

"I don't know. I don't know."

"Paula, Paula," came the chant again, "do your best. Even if you ... " The voices suddenly died away.

Paula was standing by the entrance to the ice, waiting for the signal that the girls in this flight could come on and warm up. She was wearing the turquoise, pink, and white uniform of the Marvelettes, Millwood's precision skating team. Her mother, sitting in the stands, hurried over to see what was wrong, but Paula either didn't notice or didn't want to talk to her, because she skated quickly out onto the ice to begin her warmup.

Paula was the first skater in her flight, and when the warmup was over, she skated to centre ice and took her opening pose. The strains of a Spanish trumpet played over the P.A. system, and Paula went into her program. She skated well, but somehow, whether it was a turquoise and pink costume combined with Spanish music or something was wrong with Paula, the whole thing lacked fire.

As soon as Paula came off the ice, her mother took her back into the corridor.

"Do you think she did it to make you look bad?" asked Jason. "After all, that's what seems to have happened."

"Well, if she did, how dare she?" said Angie angrily. "How dare she destroy an expensive costume like that?"

Flight One was finished, and Jennifer, in purple with bare shoulders, came out to warm up with her flight.

"Jennifer, Jennifer, jump and spin. If you try your best, then maybe you'll win!" the cheering section piped up.

Jennifer skated really well. She really was the best skater at Millwood. And her double axel was absolutely perfect.

Angie could see her mom and grandparents down at the other end of the stands, but she didn't want to go and see them right now. She wanted to get her skate over with, and then she was going to have to figure out how to deal with whatever was coming next.

It was time for Angie's flight to warm up. She stepped down from the stands and onto the ice. As she stroked around the rink, she thought about her program, she thought about the ice, she thought about skating with no boards, no boundaries. This was what she was here for. As Angie whizzed past her family, she smiled and waved to them.

"Angie, Angie, the Princess Bride," called the little girls. "If you don't win, you'll know you've tried!"

Not exactly a vote of confidence, thought Angie, as she stepped into her double axel.

10

The Motive ...

Angie landed the double axel clean, but she didn't feel sure about it. Keniesha Baker from the Minto Club in Ottawa was doing a Biellmann spin beside her. It wasn't quite the one Denise Biellmann had perfected, of course, but it was closer than Angie had ever come. Keniesha, the girl that Jason had mentioned before, looked gorgeous in a white sparkly dress that set off her dark complexion dramatically.

Ginny was right. It was kind of neat skating without boards. She felt like she might just take off and fly. There were Jennifer and Tiiu, a purple and fuchsia blur, watching the warmup. Angie wondered what Paula was telling her mother. Angie tried her layback to practise which way to come out of it. She felt a little dizzy, but remembered the blue and green wall. Oh, Angie, she muttered to herself. Focus! Focus! A long slow back spiral, getting smaller, and becoming a camel spin. Focus, focus, focus. Forget all those people on the ice, off the ice. Concentrate on skating.

The announcer cleared the ice, and Angie skated off to watch the first skaters. The first two were good enough, but Angie figured she could beat them. Then it was Keniesha's turn.

As Keniesha went through her repertoire of jumps and spins, Angie felt a little uneasy. Keniesha looked awfully good. And she landed not one, but two double axels.

Ginny was standing at Angie's elbow. "Don't worry about her," she told Angie. "She's got pep, but no finesse. Look, her elbows are all over the place."

But Angie knew that Ginny was just trying to be encouraging. Her own elbows could be all in the right place, but if she missed the double axel, it would count against her.

In what seemed like a quarter of a second, Keniesha was finished, and it was Angie's turn. She glided smoothly to centre ice, raising her arms in a graceful *port-de-bras*, stopping sharply. She took her position to begin, smiling slightly, like a princess might. The opening spiral. Footwork, jump, spin, and — the axel was in the air. Turn, turn, and ... Angie came down heavily on her right foot and wobbled a little, but she held on. After that, the rest of the program felt easy and fun.

When she came off the ice, Ginny greeted her with a hug. "See? I knew you could do it!" she was saying. Angie was soon engulfed in hugs from her mom and grandparents.

"Gran, Pops!" she greeted them.

"We couldn't find you before your skate! We wanted to wish you good luck," said Gran.

"Not that you needed it," added Pops, smiling proudly.

"Now come on, let's get a picture of you in that lovely dress," said Gran, waving around her camera. Angie glanced at her mom. Did Gran know about the dress?

"Your mom told us what a clever girl you were, fixing up your old dress," Gran went on, hustling Angie into the hallway. "I'm so proud of you, and how clever of you to put the money into extra lessons, you were just wonderful today." Angie and her mom exchanged a quick look. Gran didn't have to know there were no extra lessons, really.

"Ginny helped with the dress ..." Angie started. She didn't want to go into the hallway. She wanted to watch the other skaters in her flight. But there was no stopping Gran when she had her mind set on something. Ginny waved her away and mimed that she would watch the skaters for both of them.

Angie slipped her skateguards on and allowed herself to be dragged away, photographed, and have an orange juice bought for her while she changed out of her skates and costume. The smell of the fried foods — french fries, burgers, onion rings — was overwhelmingly tempting, but Angie knew that today was not the day to indulge, not when she had — maybe! — the finals tomorrow.

A lot of the skaters and their families were sitting around at the little tables by the snackbar. Off in one corner, she could see Paula and her mom. It was clear that Céline was angry with her daughter — probably over the costume or maybe the lifeless skate, Angie figured. Paula was still in the Marvelettes costume and her skates. Had her mom been scolding her all that time? Angie started to wonder what she should do now that she knew Paula was the culprit. Her grandparents and mom were gabbing away about something, so this was a good chance to think. Where was Jason? It would really help if she could talk it all over with him.

Soon, Céline left her daughter and walked off quickly. Paula, who had been looking very contrite, tossed her dark curly ponytail and marched over to the snack bar.

"A large fries, with gravy, and a Coke, please," Angie could hear Paula say, with a distinct note of defiance in her voice. When the order was ready, she took the tray and sat down by herself at one of the tables.

"Back in a sec," said Angie to her family, making an instant decision. She walked over to where Paula was sitting and, without asking, plonked herself down at another chair.

"Angie!" said Paula, with some surprise.

"What's going on, Paula?" Angie blurted out.

"What do you mean?"

"Why did you tear your own skating costume?"

"I did not!" exclaimed Paula.

"You did. I saw you."

"How could you see me do something I didn't do?"

Angie remembered thinking the same thing, when Jennifer told her she had proof that it was Angie who was causing all the trouble.

"Tell me if I saw this," challenged Angie. She refused to take the blame for what was happening to Paula any longer. "You went into the washroom in the dressing room. You didn't think anyone was there. You unzipped your garment bag, you took your guard off your skate, and you cut the dress with your skate. You zipped the garment bag back up, put on the guard, and hung your dress up in the dressing room, leaving it alone, so 'anyone' could have done it."

Paula was looking paler by the minute. "You weren't in the washroom," she said. "No one was. I was careful."

"So you admit that's what happened." Angie felt like Colombo or Nancy Drew right at this moment. She wished Jason were there to witness her in action.

"No — I ..." Paula stopped.

"Well, if it's not true, then what's the red thread doing on your skate guard?"

The two girls looked down at Paula's foot, and sure enough, it was still there. When they looked back at each other, Paula looked like she was going to cry.

"What business is it of yours, anyway?" she finally blurted out.

"Everyone thinks it's me. I don't like that, and it upsets *my* skating. It isn't fair."

Paula looked down at her french fries, but she didn't take one.

"Look, I'm sorry," she said at last. "I didn't mean to cause you any trouble. I didn't know it would turn out like that. I — you wouldn't understand."

"No, I doubt I would," agreed Angie. "But I think you owe me an explanation anyway."

"I want to get out of skating," Paula answered, after a moment.

Angie just stared at her. "But you're so good!"

"I don't want to be good," said Paula. "I want to have fun."

"It's not fun?" replied Angie. She could hardly get her mind around the idea.

"Oh, it's fun for you, it's fun for the others. *You* don't have 'Leger and Stein' as parents."

"I'd die to have your parents," protested Angie.

"I die having my parents," explained Paula. "I like skating, sure, but I don't want to have to live up to Canadian champions. I mean, look at that huge picture they have in the arena. It's practically suffocating. I don't like practising the same thing over and over. I don't like falling and pulling muscles. I don't like getting up at five o'clock to go to the arena and skating again at midnight. I don't like skating in competitions, I don't like having stage fright, I don't like wearing fussy costumes, I don't like wearing gloves in summer. In winter, I want to lace up my skates and go to some frozen pond with my friends and play crack the whip and have a snowball fight. And I *hate* skating pairs. It scares me to get lifted up so high."

Angie could only stare. It was like someone telling you they didn't like chocolate ice cream, though she supposed maybe somewhere there was someone who would tell her that too. "Is that why you knocked the ladder over the day Jason came?"

Paula nodded. "When you hurt yourself, it gave me the idea. I thought maybe if I hurt myself and couldn't skate, he'd just go away or get himself another partner. But I couldn't go through with it, I jumped out of the way."

"And you did all that other stuff to yourself just to get out of skating?"

"I thought if I missed enough practice time, I'd be no good, and my parents wouldn't want me to skate badly and tarnish the family name."

"You really twisted your ankle, though."

"Well, I slipped, and it was a bit twingey, but it wasn't that bad. Not bad enough to convince the doctor."

"What good did it do tearing your dress? You skated anyway," Angie pointed out.

"I thought I wouldn't have to. But Jennifer had her precision dress with her and absolutely insisted I wear it. What could I say? Somebody like her, she wouldn't understand."

"But why don't you just tell your parents?" What a waste, all that coaching from Céline and Bob going to someone who didn't even want it!

"You don't know them. I can't. I just can't. They figure that with genes from both of them, I should be the perfect skater. But I think I inherited all the not-skating genes they've got."

"But you can't just go on pretending forever. You've got to tell them."

"Look," said Paula. "I didn't skate very well today, I won't get into the finals. They'll have to see I'm not good enough, and let up on me."

Just then, Tiiu, Jennifer, and Jason came bustling up to their table.

"They're about to put the lists up," said Jennifer excitedly.

Tiiu glanced with surprise at Angie. "Come on, Paula, let's see how you did."

The two girls got up, and Tiiu and Jennifer sort of absorbed Paula, while Jason fell back with Angie. Paula left her fries untouched on the table.

Angie was dying to tell Jason what she and Paula had talked about, but something held her back. It wasn't hers to tell, somehow. Besides, he was mixed up in it. Maybe it was better to let things sort themselves out.

The skaters clustered around the notice board as one of the officials came over to pin up the standings. A group of younger girls started squealing and jumping up and down when they saw their names on their list near the top. Jennifer, Tiiu, Paula, and Angie waited. Jason had not yet skated.

The official came over to the board designated for the girls' event. The Flight Four list was posted. "I won't place," said Tiiu. Tiiu was fifth, out of twelve skaters. Jennifer put her arm around her.

"It's okay, really," said Tiiu. "I never expected to place. I'm just glad you guys didn't beat me!"

"And look," said Paula. "One of the judges placed you second."

Tiiu looked again. "They did? Wow!" A smile slowly crept over her face.

Flight Three was posted. Angie held her breath, and let it out slowly. She had placed second, behind Keniesha Baker, but she had placed. She was within the top three. She was into the finals.

11

The Opportunity

"Yay, Angie!" exclaimed Paula.

Tiiu gave her a doubtful look.

"Way to go, Ange!" said Jason.

Flight Two was posted, and Jennifer placed first. There were cheers again all around.

Meanwhile, Angie was quickly checking to see how she'd been placed by each of the judges. Two had placed her first. That was promising. It meant not everyone thought Keniesha was better than she was. In fact, the third-place finisher, a girl called April DaSilva, had been placed first by one of the judges.

When Flight One was posted, Angie was really curious. She knew that Paula thought she didn't want to place, but surely she secretly did want to get into the finals.

"Paula, you're in!" exclaimed Tiiu, bouncing up and down. Her friend had been placed third.

Paula grinned gamely. "Don't worry Paula," said Jennifer. "Third is good. It's all you need to get into the finals."

"I know," said Paula. Angie could hear the disappointment in Paula's voice, not at being as low as third, but at being as high.

Around her, Angie could hear other sounds of disappointment, encouragement, and excitement as other skaters checked the postings.

"Well, I'm skating soon," announced Jason. "Anyone coming to watch?"

"Of course," replied Jennifer.

"You're not right away are you?" asked Paula. "I really want to get changed."

Jason shook his head. "Take your time," he said. "You've got fifteen minutes."

Paula hurried off.

Tiiu and Jennifer started toward the rink, and Jason looked at Angie.

"I'll be there in a sec," she said to him. "I just have to, um, go to the washroom. Break a leg."

"You are coming, aren't you?"

"Of course!" she said. She knew Jason suspected that something was up, but now was not the time to talk about it.

Angie would tell her family the good news about the finals in a minute. First she had to talk to Paula. She followed her along the corridor to the change room. Since the last ladies' event of the day was being skated now, the room was deserted, except for Paula, who was on the bench, unlacing her skates.

"What are you going to do?" Angie asked, sitting on the bench next to her.

"Skate, of course," was Paula's reply.

"But, after tomorrow? You can't go on, if you don't like it."

"Oh, sooner or later, I'll mess up, and my parents will get the idea. In fact, I'll probably mess up tomorrow."

"No you won't," said Angie. "You'll be great!"

Paula smiled a half-smile. "No, I think I'll mess up." It was a decision, not a prediction.

Angie shook her head. "You can't go out on a bad skate," she said. "Everyone will think you're a quitter. You've got to skate your best, then tell your folks the truth."

"But don't you get it? They'll kill me!"

"Better they kill you outright than slowly kill you with misery. Anyway, they won't actually *kill* you. But keeping skating when you don't want to might."

Paula looked at Angie for a long moment.

"If you go out on a great skate," Angie pressed on, "then people will know it's your real decision, not just cowardice."

"I don't even have a costume," protested Paula, but Angie knew she was winning.

"Oh yes you do. We can salvage it. Look at what I did with mine."

"Yours? It's nice. What did you do with it?"

Angie started to speak, then thought the better of it. "Oh, it's complicated. I'll explain it all another time. We've got to go watch Jason."

On the way to the stands, the girls ran into Angie's mom and grandparents.

"Where have you been, Angie? We've been looking all over!" cried Gran. "You're in the final, oh, we're so proud of you, hon." Gran encased her in a huge hug.

"I know, Gran, but we have to go watch Jason skate now."

"Who's this Jason?" asked Gran conspiratorially, as the little group made their way to the stands.

Naturally, Jason made it to his final, too. Nearly half of the boys did, if only because there were a lot fewer of them.

"Now, Angie," said Gran, as they were standing in the foyer of the arena after the competition, "we're ordering in a pizza tonight for you and your mom. Would you like to bring your friends along?"

"I don't think — " Angie couldn't imagine inviting people over to her teeny apartment, not rich kids like Paula, anyway. But what about Paula's dress? Angie couldn't imagine why she should care, since Paula certainly hadn't cared what happened to Angie. But yet, somehow, she did. "Well, could Paula come?"

"Sure," said Gran, "They can all come! We'll get an extra-large."

"No," said Angie. "Just Paula."

"Okay," said Gran. "Just Paula. Go see if she can."

***

They'd finished the pizza, and though Paula had been shy and nervous at first, she soon relaxed around chatty Gran. The girls disappeared into Angie's room — which wasn't *too* much of a mess today — to see what they could do about Paula's dress.

"Before we get to the dress, something's been bugging me," said Angie. "You told me about the ladder and your ankle, and I get the dress and the laces and the skates. But what about the hole in your tights?"

"That was just a hole in my tights," said Paula. "It wasn't part of it."

"Oh," said Angie. "Well, let's look at this dress."

"You know, Angie?" said Paula tentatively. "It's really nice of you to help me out like this. I always thought you were a snob. But you aren't."

"You thought *I* was a snob?" snorted Angie.

Paula looked surprised. "What, you thought *I* was?"

The two girls started to laugh. It was a long time since Angie had really laughed. It felt good.

"Now about this dress … " said Angie, when they had settled down.

The dress was red, with long sleeves puffed at the top. Black lace covered the puffs and the wrists and the edge of the skirt, with the red fabric shining through. The same black lace came in a V down the front and back. It was the front V that was slashed. Angie could not see a way to fix the dress.

"We'll have to ask Gran," said Angie. "Mom can't sew, but Gran's a whiz."

"But —" Paula started to protest.

"We'll make something up," said Angie, leading the way into the living room.

"Do you have any black fabric?" asked Gran, when she had examined the dress. "I can't fix the red without it looking ragged, but the lace could be sort of fixed. And if it's over black, it won't show. I could sew in a piece of black."

"It has to stretch," said Paula.

"Hm," said Gran.

"My old black dress!" exclaimed Angie. "It's way too small!"

Paula looked like she didn't believe her. "Trust me," said Angie. "It's at that point that every time you land a jump you have to yank it down to cover your bum."

Paula still looked doubtful.

"You know I wouldn't sacrifice a dress if it were salvagable," Angie said. And that was when she told Paula about her blue dress and its origins.

"In a way, it seems fair," said Paula. "You get a dress from me, and I get a dress from you." Then she looked down. "Except I was the one who wrecked both dresses. I've wrecked everything."

"You have not," said Angie. "You can still skate your best tomorrow. And the great thing is, you don't care if you win."

***

Angie was in the dressing room in her princess dress with the sparkly beads and tulle, the shimmery tights, and the rosebud hair tie. She laced her skates up, two hooks at a time, for luck.

The door burst open, and a giggling bunch of girls wafted in, Jennifer in her purple competition dress, Tiiu in jeans and a pink sweatshirt — even though she wasn't skating today, her ultra-blond hair was still pulled back in a bun — and Paula in striking red with black lace.

Paula flounced down on the bench beside Angie. "Angie, I have told all, except to my parents. They find out tonight."

Tiiu gave Angie a tight smile. Tiiu may have owed Angie an apology, but Angie could see she wasn't going to get one.

Jennifer was more generous. "I'm sorry for yelling at you. But you'd still better never say anything about Kevin."

Angie shrugged. Why would she tell, anyway?

"The little kids are going to start in a minute," said Paula. "Come on out and watch. Jason's saving us a seat."

Angie found herself tucked between Jason and Paula. Just as the first little skater was taking the ice, Jason leaned over and squeezed her arm. "Paula told me," he whispered. "You're a really nice person, you know."

Angie felt a funny jolt go through her, but she only managed to give Jason a quick smile before the first skater's music began.

After the little girls, there were dance couples, then some slightly older girls. A very small group of young boys competed. One was outstanding, the others were okay. When the pairs came on, Jason leaned across Angie to say to Paula, "Too bad we couldn't have been ready for this competition." Paula smiled, but when Jason leaned back, he quietly added, "Or any."

Soon it was Jason's category, the second last. Jason was good, but somehow, Angie thought he looked better when he was skating with Paula. He looked like a bit was missing when he skated alone. As soon as Jason had finished, the twelve girls who were competing in the final clattered out of the stands and down to the corridor to stretch a little. Now that they were rivals, they didn't talk much. Everyone was getting nervous. Angie put her foot as high as she could on the wall and leaned into it to stretch the muscles. As she rested there, with her eyes closed, she went through her program in her mind. First, the long, slow, spiral ...

12

The Finals

Jason, as it turned out, came second. Then it was time for the final big event of the day — and Angie's chance at the scholarship money. The twelve girls skated onto the ice for their warmup, stroking around the ice, faster and faster, a whirl of colours: midnight blue, purple, red, pearly white, lime green, black, emerald green, fuchsia, powder blue, glitter, neon, floral, tan.

Angie practised her spiral, her spins, and reminded herself about the blue and green wall after the layback. She could see Ginny, Mom, Gran and Pops, and Jason in the audience, as well as Tiiu, Céline, Bob, and everyone else from Millwood. The little girls, obviously not wanting to play favourites, had a new cheer. "Millwood, Millwood Skating Club, you are super, the others are sub!"

Angie tried the easier jumps, and they felt good, they felt centred and sharp. If only she could shake the nerves that were starting to creep up the back of her neck. She breathed in slowly and out slowly. The jitters receded a little.

Angie tried the axel, just a single at first. It was fine. She wasn't going to look at any of the other skaters, she wasn't going to try to guess how they were doing today, just skate. Try the double, see how it feels. Left foot, and up, and turn, turn, and down on the right foot, not too bad. She'd have liked to have felt better about it, but it was okay. Try it again, she thought. Still not bad. Okay, don't push it, third time lucky, right? Save that for the show.

April DaSilva, the girl who had placed third in Angie's flight yesterday, skated first. She took the ice, looking very appealing in powder blue with a traily skirt. Her number was sexy, but April herself seemed uncomfortable with the sexiness. Technically, she was good, though. The girl in the flower print was next.

Shaking out her legs, Paula turned to Angie. "Thanks, you know. I'm not even nervous today."

"Lucky you," said Angie.

"Yeah, well, I've always got my lucky button," grinned Paula. She slipped a piece of black elastic with a button on it from her wrist. "It's all that's left of my old lucky dress — the one I landed my first axel in." She held it out to Angie. "Here, you wear it for your skate. Maybe it will bring you luck too."

Angie looked at Paula. She couldn't believe a competitor — actually, a rival! — was lending her a lucky charm. "Don't you want it?"

"Nah," Paula tossed off. "I don't need to be lucky today. I'm just going to go out and forget everything and have fun. I know my muscles know the moves."

"Thanks," Angie replied quietly, as she slipped the elastic over her wrist. It couldn't be seen below the tulle ruffle.

"No problem. Wish me luck," finished Paula, as she skated out for her program.

As the Spanish trumpets blared out Paula's opening, and the manic guitars took up the rhythm, Angie watched Paula. She was good, she was so good. Why would she want to give all this up? She really was like a Spanish dancer, all flashing eyes, and Angie would have sworn she had castanets if she didn't know better. But then Paula's jumps began. She had height, but she popped every one of them and they ended up being singles. The number looked flashy, and Paula looked like she was having fun, but it was all show. There! Half the combination jump was a simple waltz jump. And then Paula's dramatic, abrupt finish. The crowd cheered, but Angie knew the judges were marking her down on those jumps. What would Paula's parents say?

Paula came off the ice and went immediately to get water, but not before flashing Angie a breathless smile. That comment about forgetting everything and having fun tickled the edge of Angie's consciousness. If Paula could have that much fun out there, why couldn't she?

Jennifer was on the ice now, with her languorous, dreamy opening to music from *Swan Lake*. Angie couldn't help thinking how interesting it was to do *Swan Lake* and not get dressed up as a swan, like Oksana Baiul. Jennifer was terrific, as always. Nothing ever seemed to affect her concentration.

Another girl did a number to the music from the *Pocahontas* movie, which had some interesting and unusual choreography, but not a lot of sparkle.

Keniesha was a firecracker, but, like Ginny said, all pizzazz and no finesse. Still, judges liked that sort of thing too.

Finally, it was Angie's turn. Just like yesterday, she glided gracefully to centre ice. The familiar mandolin from *The Princess Bride* began, and she stepped into the long, slow spiral. Hips forward, leg high, you're a bird, Angie. The flashy footwork, light on her feet, now. In her mind's eye, Angie could see the light flashing off her blades. Then a beautiful spreadeagle, sharp as a paper cut. Angie started to smile for real now, flashing not just her "show" smile. She was remembering why she was here — because she loved to skate. Because she loved to leap through the air as though there were no gravity, as though she were a cloud that sailed through the sky. And all the scholarships in the world wouldn't change that, and if they made her tense and miserable, as she had been so often in the past months, she didn't want them anyway. Here comes the double axel. Step, jump, and she was up. She felt like she had been yanked up by a wire. In mid-air, she turned, and again, and a half, and finally she floated down onto her right back outside edge, and it was perfect. She had let go of the jump in her mind, and it had found her.

***

Angie was still spinning as she lay in bed that night. She couldn't possibly sleep after all the excitement. Ginny told her she nearly gave her heart failure — she had gone into that jump with so much abandon, she thought Angie would land spinning and fall. Gran told her (again!) how proud she was, and Mom hugged her a million times. Céline and Bob, later on, asked her it she would consider trying out with Jason for pairs. Paula had told her to keep the lucky button.

"I don't need it any more," Paula had pointed out. "Since I'm only going to skate for fun."

But Angie insisted on giving it back. "It's your lucky button. And it was your joy in skating, and your good advice that helped me, not the button, anyway."

"Not to mention your hard work," Paula pointed out.

This all happened when everyone was out to dinner — Paula's family and Angie's family and Jason's family, who were all together for the competition. They were so many in the Chinese restaurant that they got to sit at one of the big round tables with a lazy Susan in the middle and spin it around to get their food. Angie realized that she had taken the first of many steps into her future. Maybe, just maybe, those steps would lead up an Olympic podium someday. It was all like some magical dream.

But the way the moonlight glinted off the gold medal propped up on Angie's dresser tonight, that was no dream.